Frederick George Jackson, Helen Peel, Joseph Wiggins

Polar Gleams

An Account of a Voyage on the Yacht 'Blencathra'

Frederick George Jackson, Helen Peel, Joseph Wiggins

Polar Gleams
An Account of a Voyage on the Yacht 'Blencathra'

ISBN/EAN: 9783337396442

Printed in Europe, USA, Canada, Australia, Japan

Cover: Foto ©Andreas Hilbeck / pixelio.de

More available books at **www.hansebooks.com**

POLAR GLEAMS

AN ACCOUNT OF A VOYAGE

ON THE

YACHT 'BLENCATHRA'

BY

HELEN PEEL

WITH A PREFACE BY

THE MARQUESS OF DUFFERIN AND AVA

AND CONTRIBUTIONS BY

CAPTAIN JOSEPH WIGGINS AND FREDERICK G. JACKSON

LONDON

EDWARD ARNOLD, 37 BEDFORD STREET, W.C.

𝔓𝔲𝔟𝔩𝔦𝔰𝔥𝔢𝔯 𝔱𝔬 𝔱𝔥𝔢 𝔍𝔫𝔡𝔦𝔞 𝔒𝔣𝔣𝔦𝔠𝔢

1894

AFFECTIONATELY DEDICATED

TO MY FATHER,

Sir Robert Peel,

IN DELIGHTFUL REMEMBRANCE

OF A CRUISE

THROUGH ARCTIC SEAS.

PREFATORY NOTE

In entrusting the frail bark of a first literary effort to an ocean more formidable than the storm-abounding Arctic Sea, I shall reasonably incur the charge of rashness.

As every effort, however, must have a beginning, I can only prefix a few words of explanation to my attempt, and tender an apology for inviting public notice to a book which, I am painfully aware, can pretend to no literary excellence, but which, I trust, will be judged in the same indulgent spirit that the House of Commons extends to a "maiden speech."

In the compilation of the following pages, I desired to guide my indulgent friends and readers over comparatively unknown waters to the mighty

Yenesei River, which issues from a region associated in the popular mind with much that is horrible in climatic severity, and repugnant owing to its being pictured as a gigantic and cruel prison-house for political exiles; but this river is destined to become one of the great highways of the world.

The ideas generally held of the great continent of Siberia are in many respects erroneous. Travellers of renown have lately given to us their personal experience of this immense country and its infinite resources, and have thus helped to dispel misconceptions and allay a tendency to exaggerate obstacles to its development. Siberia is at present undergoing a complete transformation through the increased facilities of navigation along its mighty rivers, and the creation of the great railway now under construction by the enterprise of the Russian Government. It would be difficult to exaggerate the importance of this development.

The first nine chapters of my book give a slight narrative of my voyage through arctic waters. These are kindly supplemented with an account by Captain Wiggins of his homeward journey through Siberia, after he parted from the *Blencathra* at Golchika to proceed up the Yenesei ; and he also adds, at my request, some notes on Dr. Nansen's expedition. These arctic experiences are finally wound up in Chapter XII. by a letter from Mr. Jackson, with a sketch of the plan for his projected exploration and, if possible, arrival at the North Pole, where it is his patriotic ambition to be the first to plant the standard of his native land and sing "God save the Queen."

HELEN PEEL.

PREFACE

BY THE MARQUESS OF DUFFERIN AND AVA

WHEN my eldest son was a child of six or seven, he slipped on the ice in a Canadian rink, and broke a front tooth. After picking him up and assuaging his tears, I asked him what had brought about the catastrophe. He replied, " Papa, I was running after a little girl." Seeking, like a prudent parent, to improve the occasion, I told him that this should be a lesson to him for the rest of his life, as one always comes to grief when "one runs after a little girl."

The echo of this excellent advice recurred to my memory as I was drawn by the interest of her narrative to follow my godchild, Miss Helen Peel, on her voyage past Cape Wrath, the Shetland

Islands and the North Cape, into the misty terrors of the Kara Sea. I remember, as a yachtsman, thinking it something of an achievement getting as far as Iceland and the Lofoden Islands; but here is a young lady who carries us off to Lapland, Waigatz Straits, the northern coasts of Asia, and half way through the north-west passage, besides casting an occasional sheep's-eye at the North Pole. Moreover, so far from her corsage consisting of "oak and three-fold brass," as the ingenuous Horace imagined, our authoress seems to have left her sealskin jacket behind her, and to have graced the Arctic Circle in a frock of Cowes serge. That a last year's débutante should thus exchange the shining floors, wax lights, and valses of a London ball-room for the silent shores of Novaia Zemlia and the Taimyr Peninsula, with their accompaniments of ice-floes and winds fresh from the cellars of Boreas, exhibits the untamable audacity of our modern maidens. However, she seems to have been quite satisfied with

the company she found in these shivering
regions, in the shape of walruses and uncon-
ventional Samoyedes ;

> Quae siccis oculis monstra natantia
>
> . . . vidit . . . . et
>
> Infames scopulos Nordokeraunia.

In vain, indeed, as Horace adds, " has a prudent
Deity cut off such lands by the unsociable ocean,
if the impious yachts " of these young women thus
disquiet their hyperborean solitudes ! Nevertheless, having once taken the plunge, no one will
regret following in the wake of the *Blencathra*
from the old-world Elizabethan port of Appledore
to the mouths of the Mongolian Yenesei, under
the auspices of so enthusiastic and cheerful a
Minerva, who revels in the discomforts of the
North Sea as likely to give greater zest to future
joys, and remains philosophically in bed while her
ship runs aground on a sand-bank. Once only,
I observe, does her stoicism falter, when, in order
to save her own, she threw her arms round the

neck of her skin-clad Jehu, as she bumped over brake and boulder at the tail of a team of madcap Siberian reindeer.

In spite of these palpitating experiences, or perhaps by reason of them, after what appears to have been a delightful cruise, which has made us appreciate better than ever the great benefits rendered to commerce by her gallant companion and fellow-navigator, Captain Wiggins, Miss Peel sails back out of the mists of the north, reinvigorated in mind and body, and endeavours in these pages to brighten our stay-at-home dulness with the stored-up radiance of her midnight suns.

CONTENTS

CHAPTER IX

CHAPTER X

Contributed by Captain Joseph Wiggins.

CHAPTER XI

CHAPTER XII

APPENDIX A

APPENDIX B

LIST OF ILLUSTRATIONS

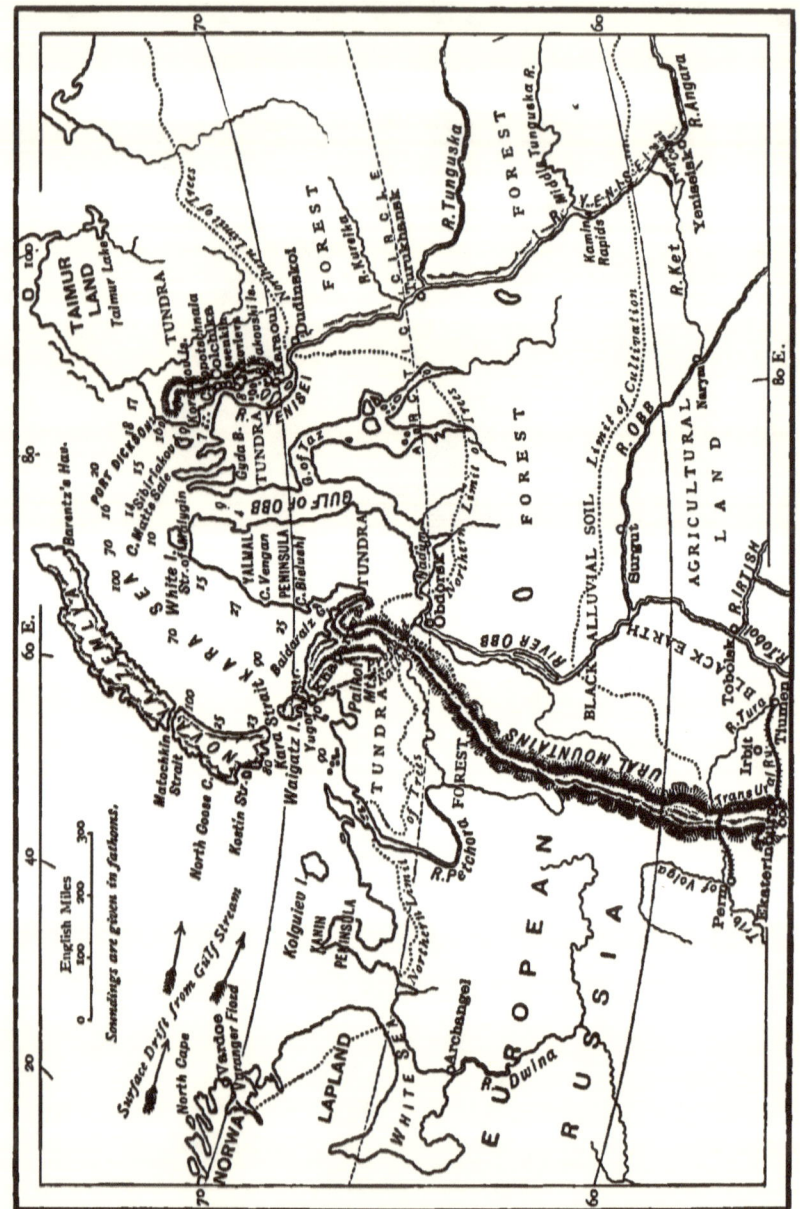

Sea Route to Siberia.

CHAPTER I

SHE is off to the North Pole! was the ex-
clamation of my friends, as I left London on
the 18th of July 1893, bound for Siberia, the
grim and rueful land of many sorrows, as we
have learned to think of it.

Youth and love of adventure inspired me
with a longing for new experiences, regardless
of unforeseen perils and friendly warnings.

I only felt elated with the thought of a visit
to arctic regions, unlike all that I had hitherto
seen and enjoyed in fairer climes.

The terrors of the sea to an inexperienced

B

and bad sailor are no doubt formidable drawbacks, but they were overborne, as were all
other anticipated dangers, by a weird resistless
impulse to sail through the icebergs of the
Kara Sea, up the mighty Yenesei River, and to
be the first of my sex to do so. All this was
sufficient to determine me to accept an invitation for such an enterprise; even though we
should not exactly reach the goal of so much
ambition, and solve the problem whether or
not we might feast on strawberries and cream
at the North Pole.

The object of this important expedition, under
contract with the Russian Government, was to
take a cargo of 1600 tons of rails for the Great
Siberian Railway, in course of construction,
which will probably occupy twelve years to
build, and entail the enormous expenditure of
350 million roubles for the seven Cheliabinsk-
Vladivostock sections. Its total lengths, reckon-
ing from Libau on the shores of the Baltic Sea
to Vladivostock on the Pacific coast, will be over
some 7000 miles, and, when complete, will form

a continuous iron girdle of railway communication encircling the whole earth. The Czarevitch
cut the first sod at Vladivostock on the 24th of
May 1891. In reality the Great Siberian Railway
embraces a very wide zone, the enormous area
exceeding the whole extent of central Europe,
Germany, Austro-Hungary, Holland, Belgium,
and Denmark, and the route chosen connecting
the extensive basins of such large rivers as the
Obi, Yenesei, Amour, and part of the Lena. It
is difficult for the imagination to conceive the
immense extent of the earth's surface, hitherto
scarcely known or recognised, which will be
opened up by this great railroad, or what pro-
gressive impetus may be given to international
commercial enterprise by the development of
such great sources of wealth, and consequent
happiness, to overgrown populations.

To the great nation in whose sovereignty these
new territories are comprised, the railway will
certainly bring increased political importance, and
no doubt they will prove to be of service to other
nations, as well indeed to mankind in general, not

much less than to the people by whose energy and public spirit they have, one may truly say, been just called into existence. The prosperity of one people, rightly understood and used, will turn out to be the prosperity of all others brought into mutual commercial relations with them, in which colonisation will no doubt play an important part.

Accordingly a small fleet of three vessels was fitted out. The arctic steam-yacht *Blencathra* was to act as convoy to the *Orestes*, a large powerful steamer of 2500 tons' burden on light draught, chartered from London for the purpose of conveying rails to Siberia, with another steel shallow draught steam-yacht to carry 250 tons' cargo and some gold-mining machinery. This latter vessel was called the *Minusinsk*, after a city situated on the Yenesei River, being one of the Nijni Novgorods of Siberia for trading in grains, etc.

In addition to this little fleet we were to be joined at Vardoe, in North Norway, by three steamers, under the command of Russian officers

of the Imperial Navy. Their vessels, built at
Dumbarton on the Clyde, consisted of a twin-
screw steamer, *Lieutenant Offtzine*, under the
command of Lieutenant Dobrotvorscy ; a paddle-
steamer, *Lieutenant Malyguine*, under the command of Lieutenant Svede ; and a schooner-barge,
Scuratoff, commanded by Lieutenant Sunderman.

These vessels were entirely manned by Russian
naval officers and sailors, with Russian engineers.

This imposing fleet of six vessels was to form
the most important expedition that had ever
crossed the much dreaded Kara Sea, and the rails
taken by the *Orestes* were to be the first cargo
of such heavy material ever conveyed by sea to
Siberia.

We may now confidently expect to find a regular
yearly service between England and Siberia fully
established, and doubtless in time a trade of
considerable dimensions will grow up. For the
natural wealth of Siberia is well known to be
enormous, and, apart from this, the sea route is
open to navigation two to three months or more
out of the twelve.

Bideford, pleasantly situated in the delicious scenery of North Devon, was the place of our "rendezvous" and five days' stay. It is far too remarkable, alike for its history and unequalled attractions, to need any introductory notice, for who has not read Kingsley's *Westward Ho!* a tale so closely associated with the old town ? At an early period Bideford had achieved fame. In Elizabethan and Stuart times it was one of the chief naval and commercial ports of England ; and among the first settlers of Virginia and Carolina were Sir Walter Raleigh and other distinguished heroes of that town.

We lost no time wandering over the exquisite country of which Clovelly and Westward Ho are in themselves delightful attractions, fanned by the fresh ocean breeze of the Atlantic.

In the conference room of the Royal Hotel, which dates from 1688, we discussed our arctic expedition with Captain Joseph Wiggins, the well-known Sunderland navigator, whose name and established reputation are widely recognised. Discoverer of the ocean route to Siberia in 1874, he is a man of great nautical experience and genius, and of delightful conversational powers ; his characteristic physique testifies to an enterprising nature, and to thorough acquaintance with the perils and dangers of arctic sea life.

Captain Wiggins impressed me at once, and filled us all with such unbounded confidence that, had the most perilous circumstances arisen, we should have placed ourselves unreservedly under his command.

My first acquaintance with the ship, which was to be my home for so many months, took place on the 20th of July. It was anchored some two miles above the bar, at the meeting of the Torridge and the Taw, off the little white fishing village of Appledore, which is associated with an interesting historical fact, being the port from which King Alfred destroyed the Danish fleet in 894.

All who are interested in yachting have no doubt heard of the old *Pandora*, built in 1867 as a gunboat, and then purchased by Sir Allan Young. Her name was then changed into that of *Blen-*

cathra, the name of a mountain in Cumberland, by the present owner, Mr. F. Leybourne Popham, to whom I am not only indebted for this interesting cruise but for several months of kind hospitality.

The *Blencathra* is a three-master rigged schooner, 424 tons, 146 feet long, 25 feet broad, 12 feet depth, and being a vessel intended for arctic seas she is entirely built of wood, and was fitted with an ice-ram in anticipation of the impediments to free progress in the Kara Sea.

Her deck cabins constituted her great charm; they included four comfortable berths, with bath-rooms, and the main cabin, in which most of our days were spent, was furnished both with a piano and an organum, the attractions of which, during the whole of the voyage, were of never-failing delight. Her lower cabin was supplied with six months' stores, in view of the possibility of being nipped in the ice.

Our party consisted of two ladies and two gentlemen, and a crew numbering twenty-four.

On the 24th of July a sudden and early start was made by train to Instow. It was the

The S.S. Yacht " Blencathra."

(From a Kodak Photograph.)

To face page 8.

humour of the gentlemen who were of our party
to think and decide a course of action with impul-
sive speed. " No sooner said than done " would
have been a suitable motto. The worst of this
disposition was that the ladies were expected to
follow suit, and to pack up their numerous
impedimenta and carry out the programme set
before them with the utmost haste. In ten
minutes we were to be at the station, and the
scramble, bustle, and confusion that ensued can
be more easily imagined than described, whilst
dozens of parcels, boxes, and wraps were strewn
in untidy appearance on the platform, as we had
simply pitched everything pell - mell into our
trunks, heedless of consequences — summer
fripperies and fur - lined snowboots, mosquito
nets and hot-water bottles jostling one another
in hopeless confusion, since we were obliged
to provide ourselves alike against summer heat
and the cold of an arctic winter.

A few minutes' rail conveyed us to Instow,
from which a boat landed us on board the
Blencathra.

My first night at sea will ever remain memorable.

Everything was new and strange to me.

How small my berth looked, how unsettled I felt!

Even the invigorating freshness of the sea was scarcely relished. I began to realise that my golden anticipations would soon reveal themselves under the test of practice.

No! my heart failed me as I wondered how I could have fallen such a victim to my rashness in undertaking the enterprise. Dreams and nightmares also capped my imaginings, revealing before my eyes visions of waves mountains high, gales, polar bears, icebergs, and myself denuded of nose, ears, fingers, and toes, and consequently exiled as a recluse from all social intercourse for the rest of my days. But "nothing venture, nothing have," so I resolved to screw up my courage to the sticking point, and brave the dangers which perhaps existed only in my imagination.

CHAPTER II

AMID loud and hearty cheers the *Blencathra* weighed anchor on the 25th of July from Appledore, and at 4 P.M. successfully crossed the bar, notwithstanding the falling tide.

On reaching the open sea we encountered a heavy storm, so that scarcely had we "shaken down" when we were fairly "shaken up" again.

I did full justice to my reputation as a bad sailor, nor did I fail in this respect throughout the voyage whenever a sea got up. Our skipper, Captain Brown, a native of Dundee, took pity on me, and prescribed a bottle of Yorkshire relish, but thinking the cure worse than the complaint, I declined his offer.

For twenty-four hours we pitched and tossed considerably, but my companions, unaffected by the heavy sea into which we dived, kept the deck, and delighted in the grandeur of the stormy waters.

On the 27th of July we reached Holyhead, and, after stopping to drop our Appledore pilot, we resumed our northerly course. A dead calm prevailed, and as we coasted along we thoroughly enjoyed the wild weird scenery of Scotland's coast.

Everything was now ship-shape; we began to feel quite at home with one another, as we became inured to our surroundings and better acquainted.

At Cape Wrath, a distance of 500 miles had already been accomplished. On the 30th July we steered east of the Shetlands, and were greeted with a nasty head-wind. How we tossed and rolled again, as a plaything of the waves, reckless of our discomfort. I, with most awkward sea legs, was bruised all over. My berth happened to be a particularly wide one, a defect which greatly interfered with my sleep, for when the ship rolled heavily it was all I could do to avoid being pitched out, for to cling to both sides was a feat not easily accomplished.

On the 3rd of August we crossed the Arctic Circle, which passes through the Fraenen Island, in the meridian of 13 degrees east of Greenwich. In brilliant sunshine we distinguished the snow-capped mountains of Norway, while to our left rose the majestic peaks of the Lofoden Islands. I must here note that we had provided ourselves with a pilot from Bergen, and were thus enabled to steer at leisure into the fjords, and our course led us through the Vest Fjord, which opened out a scene of marvellous grandeur. The view was glorious — everything still and calm, even the water seemed immovable, so perfect were the reflections from the sharp outlines of the mountains.

And then from day to day new beauties revealed themselves. One of the great charms of the fjords is the uncertainty of knowing in what direction the next turn may lead, as no outlet is visible. Sometimes one passes between wild

perpendicular cliffs, again along smiling shores
fringed in the distance by well-wooded hills. It
is the wonderful blending of the gentle and peaceful with the wild, rugged yet sublime aspects of
nature which is so characteristic of Norwegian
scenery. Small villages with sparsely scattered
houses now and again dot the landscape. Built
of wood and painted terra-cotta and white, they
appear in the distance like miniature dolls' houses.

The extraordinary effects of light and shade in
these high latitudes are quite enchanting. Although we missed seeing the phenomenon of the
midnight sun, we enjoyed almost continuous daylight. It seemed so strange to think of "turning
in" while the sun was shining brightly, remind-
ing me of the late hours of London dances.

Such thoughts, however, were soon dispelled
by a further contemplation of the scenery which
surrounded us. Great was our excitement when,
for the first time since leaving Appledore, we
dropped anchor at 3.30 A.M. on the 5th of August at
Tromsoe. Nestling under the protection of high
hills, the town is situated by the water's edge, on

the east side of an island. The approach was
quite lovely. A number of fishing smacks and
walrus sloops were anchored off the beach. So
eager were we to go ashore and get a glimpse of
Norwegian life that, regardless of the hour, we
dressed and paraded the town in search of adventures: all was, however, shrouded in the dull
silence of sleep. In vain we rung at hotel doors,
every portal was locked and bolted. But after
some patient waiting there appeared signs of life.
The curiosity of the inhabitants was soon displayed. No wonder! for the tourist season was
at an end, and consequently our voices must have
sounded unfamiliar. On we walked, laughing and
joking, appearing in the stillness of the town
somewhat boisterous in our hilarity, followed by
our three dogs, whose wild spirits, in harmony
with our own, were not to be checked. We paid
no regard to the slumbering town, but we were
not to pass unperceived. Behind every shutter
lurked a nightcap, under every nightcap peered
inquisitive eyes, set in delicate pink and white
frames. Certainly their owners seemed attractive!

Finally, tired and hungry, and at the moment sorely tried by what we deemed the laziness of the inhabitants, we rowed back to the ship, to find on our return to Tromsoe, several hours later, the town presenting quite a different and most animated aspect. The gentlemen formed a Committee of Taste, to pass judgment on the young and pretty inhabitants of the town, who seemed quite to realise their expectations. It happened to be market-day, and the crowds about the market-place were great. The majority were Lapps, who in the summer time leave their encampments to purchase provisions for the winter months. The first Lapp I saw was an elderly-looking unattractive man, of very diminutive stature, and being armed with a camera I instantly fixed the lens upon him. He was quite infuriated and, I believe, thought it was some infernal machine, or that I was bringing him under some magical spell, for he squeaked and gesticulated in a very comical manner.

Unfortunately I was at a disadvantage in my interpretation of his capers and expressions of

A SNAP-SHOT AT TROMSOE.

To face page 16.

indignation. He was clothed in his winter garments, which consisted of a long tunic of reindeer skin falling just below the knees, and belted up by a leathern girdle, to which was suspended the inevitable knife, with which from time immemorial almost all Scandinavians have been armed. The lower part of the dress was a sort of legging, also made of reindeer skins. A substitute for stockings was found in the soft dried grass, called *sena*, with which the fur shoes were well stuffed, and a long narrow band was twisted several times tightly round the ankle, to prevent the possibility of any snow coming in. His headdress was a sort of cloth cap turned up all round with a facing of reindeer fur. In summer the Lapps wear a dark blue homespun cloth dress decorated with bright colours, which have special attractions for them, and coming as we did between the cold and warm season, we saw both these characteristic toilettes. On wedding and feast days in particular they display most gaudy attires. It is this variety of colour which makes the Lapland costumes so very picturesque.

C

The women are very like the men, both in aspect and costume, in fact I could hardly tell the difference between them. The average height rarely exceeds 5 feet. They have small elongated eyes, high cheek-bones, tanned complexions, and their hair is generally of a dark colour. A few sparse hairs constitute the beards of the men, which are thus almost imperceptible. The baby Lapps are wrapped in their cradles like little mummies.

The origin of the Lapps is somewhat obscure, but they seem to be closely connected with the Samoyedes and Eskimos. They depend to some extent upon the reindeer for sustenance as well as for locomotion ; moreover, nature is so bountiful in providing fish that the Lapps are thus also liberally supplied. They have large encampments in a neighbouring valley, which it would have been interesting to visit, but as time pressed we were unable to do so.

At the Russian consulate we engaged two ice-masters for the Kara Sea, and attracted much interest and curiosity by the rumour of our intended cruise to Siberia. The fact of English ladies venturing through the Kara Sea, willing to encounter obstacles and even perils, with nothing apparently to tempt them but adventure, quite staggered them, and we were no doubt instantly put down as mad and eccentric English-women, not likely to be heard of again.

The Norwegians struck me by their likeness to the English, the women more especially so. With very fair hair and blue eyes, they have fine profiles and elongated faces, with fresh pink and white complexions. The universal head-dress is a plain or coloured handkerchief tied under the chin in a most becoming fashion. The Nor-wegians looked serious and sombre, with nothing of the vivacity of the children of a southern clime.

Drunkenness is a vice almost unknown to them. I noticed their beautiful little horses, which in size are really more like ponies. They appear to be in good condition and very gentle in temper, probably from the fact of being well cared for and kindly treated, whips, I am told, being rarely used in Norway, while their harness is most primitive, though embracing all essentials.

Meanwhile the *Blencathra* had been stocked with fresh provisions, and at 1 P.M. we returned on board, delighted with our morning gleanings. Two hours later we weighed anchor, steaming through scenery simply superb. Such a moving panorama can, I am sure, rarely be met with. So once again we directed our course toward the North.

The next harbour touched at was Hammerfest, a nice clean-looking place, very modern in appearance, from the fact of its having, some four years ago, been completely destroyed by fire and consequently rebuilt; its surroundings are extremely barren, hardly a shrub to be seen, and only rocks piled upon each other. We lowered the boats and rowed ashore, intending to ship another ice-master. The pier was crowded with small boys and girls, who followed our steps in such numbers that we wondered what freak the high latitudes had worked in our outward appearance. The Russian Consul having been called out of

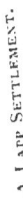

A LAPP SETTLEMENT.

To face page 46.

church to satisfy our inquiries, we heard that our third ice-master had left the day before to join us at Vardoe.

Hammerfest, on closer inspection, revealed nothing of interest; but it has a well-sheltered harbour, in which floated several Russian fishing-smacks from the White Sea, from whence they carry on an active trade. The air was pervaded with a strong smell of cod-liver and train oil, a faint foretaste of the putrid atmosphere we were about to inhale at Vardoe; so with nothing to tempt us ashore we returned on board the *Blencathra*, bidding farewell to the most northern town in the world. It certainly seemed strange to realise that in a few hours we were to find ourselves in the same latitude as the island of Jan Mayen.

CHAPTER III

NORTHWARD HO !

Yes, indeed, I felt very much like going towards the mysterious Pole as we sailed from Hammerfest out of reach of civilised life, away from all turmoil and feverish bustle, to the land of the midnight sun and the aurora borealis. Curious sensations took possession of me, most difficult to describe. I felt stimulated by the thought of unknown regions, and excited by the exhilarating air, which seemed not only to purify one's thoughts, but also helped to brush away conventional cobwebs from the brain.

As we advanced, the coast scenery towards the North Cape became wilder and more desolate. The mountains present themselves with more deterring ruggedness and become strikingly Alpine in character, bringing home to me panoramas of Swiss scenery, familiar from childhood.

What a delightful prospect in view for tourists, to whom this wild scenery is yet unknown. Variety of form and outline is here displayed at every new turn, scene upon scene following each other with such rapidity that one never gets tired of gazing, but, on the contrary, one's interest increases. Often, as I sat up on deck, I felt inclined to regret not being endowed with the talent of an artist. What a region indeed for the painter's brush! How glorious the colouring!

Instead of rounding the North Cape we steamed through a narrow fjord between the mainland of Finmark and the wild-looking island of Mageröe, in which is situated the North Cape. It seemed disappointing at first, but, as it turned out, we enjoyed a far finer view of these dark perpendicular headlands decked in winter's garb on our return voyage.

It became very cold as we steamed along the northern coast of Finmark, and was raining heavily. Several little red-poles flew on board and settled on the rigging. We happened to have an owl, brought with the purpose of introducing it into Siberia, and a shivering little red-pole was unmercifully caught alive and given to the owl, who instantly attempted to swallow it, feathers and all. Arriving on the scene at that moment, my indignation was aroused by this act of cruelty. However, the owl's position was at the same time extremely comical—there it stood, half choking, with open beak and only the bird's tail showing. At last after a deal of effort the tail disappeared, but fairly did for the owl, who died next day.

At last we came in view of Vardoe, a goal we had been ardently looking forward to. On the 7th of August we dropped anchor inside the harbour, among quite a fleet of fishing boats and sailing vessels. We found the *Minusinsk*, one of the ships which formed part of our fleet through the Kara Sea, awaiting our arrival. The three

Russian ships were still on their way north from Dumbarton, and the *Orestes*, under the command of Captain Wiggins, was expected from day to day. The harbour-master came on board, and after all the usual formalities had been observed, we went ashore in a pouring rain to get letters and send telegrams, and make the acquaintance of the British Vice-Consul, who in nationality is a Norwegian.

Vardoe, where we spent more than a fortnight, requires only a few words to render its description complete.

Forming an H-shaped island, situated at some distance from the Varanger Fjord, the town consists of wooden houses clustering round the harbour. None are more than two storeys high, as a precaution against the violence of the gales. I noticed most of the roofs were of turf, with such lovely green grass that goats are to be seen grazing away on the top of them. Such a novel effect !

The old castle of Vardoehüüs, the most northerly fort in Europe, is the one object of slight interest.

To return, however, to Vardoe's chief characteristic.   Any one who has been there will
undoubtedly associate it with terrible odours, to
put it mildly, although a stronger and more
vulgar appellation would be much more to the
point, for the air is simply saturated with the
smell of fish, in almost every stage of decomposition, in fact Vardoe may be said to be almost
made up of wooden frames, on which are hung
to dry in the sun thousands upon thousands of
fish and cods' heads, the latter for sale, and to be
exported as guano.

The harbour is made very lively with troops
of fishermen, who carry on an enormous trade.
The crafts from the White Sea particularly
attracted my attention, not from a fishing or a
nasal point of view, but from the fact of the
Russian fishermen being so extremely handsome
and kind-looking as to excite my admiration, a
weakness which on future acquaintance with
Russians only increased, for being tall and well-
built, with full long fair beards, they present a
striking appearance in their pink worsted shirts.

LAPPS.

To face page 26.

The fortnight spent at Vardoe was anything but pleasant, nothing but smell, cold, and rain. We made the best of it, however.

One Sunday morning we attended divine service in the Norwegian Church, conducted after the Lutheran system. The fashion is curious. One aisle is reserved for the women, the other one occupied by men. The pastor was robed in a black gown with a white ruff-collar, recalling the fashion of Queen Elizabeth's time. The rapidity of his delivery was astonishing, and as not a word of what he said was understood by us, we grew extremely impatient. But that was not all. The majority of men were Lapps and fishermen, who imparted to us every variety of smell, which they abundantly wafted from their clothes and persons. No sooner was the sermon over than we made a rush for the door, to escape from this poisonous atmosphere.

One day we sallied forth on a fishing expedition, having previously engaged two Norwegian fishermen to show us how the trade was carried on. Accordingly we steamed off in the *Minu-*

sinsk, and towed at the same time out of the harbour a large Russian cargo boat, whose crew—it being only a sailing vessel—had been waiting for more than three weeks for a breeze, and were deeply grateful to us for our help.

Some few miles off the coast we dropped our trawls, which were short lines with 1200 baited hooks attached to them. Leaving them for a few hours, we steamed on and began fishing merely with bright hooks, pulling them up and down as fast as we could. A kind of reel was fastened to the side of the ship, thus facilitating the hauling up of cod, haddock, halibut, plaice, etc. Most of them weighed as much as twenty pounds, and a gaff had to be used to haul them up. So numerous were they that scarcely had we dropped our hooks than we felt a fish rushing to meet its fate. The sport was most exciting, and the number of fish caught almost too great to be believed.

Returning towards evening to pick up our trawls, we found very nearly every hook occupied,—a strange sight. In fact the little rowing boat was quite weighed down by them, so that the slightest misadventure might have capsized it. The water is simply alive with fish, and consequently the price of the largest cod or haddock hardly ever exceeds a penny.

On another occasion we visited the whaling station at some short distance from Vardoe, and, as luck would have it, a large whale happened to be towed in behind a small whaling steamer. They are now captured by means of explosive shells. We landed to have a look over the factories, determined to brave the terrible nauseous obstacle, which to windward was something dreadful. The processes of manufacture which the poor dead body of the whale has to undergo before being ready for shipment is astonishing. After almost every part of the body has been made use of, the carcasses are left on the beach in a state of decomposition, waiting to be shipped for uses similar to that of guano. It is this which infects the air for miles around.

On the 7th of August we found the *Orestes* anchored in the harbour. Captain Wiggins had

arrived during the night straight from Middles-
borough, having as a passenger a young Englishman, Mr. Jackson. His object was to take
advantage of our voyage through the Kara Sea
to get dropped on the coast of the Yalmal Peninsula, for the purpose of exploring the interior.

Overmastered by the idea of being the first
to fly the Union Jack from the North Pole, and
exasperated at the thought of the probable success of Dr. Nansen depriving him of the glory in
view, he resolved to spend the winter in these
high latitudes in order to get acclimatised to the
rigour of arctic temperature, and to prepare himself for the feat of hoisting the British flag on
the North Pole in the event of its being unoccu-
pied by the flag of Norway.

On the 17th August great excitement was
caused at Vardoe by the arrival of the Russian
naval officers on board three light draught
steamers, which had just been built on the Clyde
for Siberian river-work. They consisted of a
paddle-boat, a screw, and a schooner, and were
under the command of Lieutenant Dobrotvorscy.

SKINNING A WHALE AT VARDOE

To face page 3

Anxious to make their acquaintance, we proposed to give a dinner party. At 7.30 P.M. we sat down to a merry repast, and among the invited were Lieutenant Dobrotvorscy; Mr. Holmboe, the Russian Vice-Consul, and his cousin Miss Holmboe; Mr. Bereniskoff, the Russian Consul-General, and Dr. Bunge, who has acquired great distinction by his scientific inquiries into the history of the mammoths during his five years' stay on the desolate New Siberian Islands. I was delighted with the company; they struck me as being extremely amiable and full of kindness, and we very soon made closer and more familiar acquaintance. After dinner we had music, followed next night by another entertainment on a larger scale. Ten officers came to spend the evening, and some of them joined their musical capacities to ours, so that besides having a piano and an organum, a violin and a flute, we had the mandolin, guitar, and human voices. It was difficult to conceive our not being in familiar surroundings instead of on the threshold of Polar Seas.

The Russian Consul was a great character, tall and strongly built, and full of humour. One Sunday we went in a little steam-launch to inspect the rocky island of Hornö, situated to the right of Vardoe, taking the Consul with us. The sea was very rough, and the waves quite alarmed me. We landed on the island, teeming with sea-birds of all kinds, which filled the air with their incessant cries. Never had I seen such numbers of gulls and eider ducks. After much exertion we climbed to the top of the rocks, which are entirely devoid of any shrubs, commanding a splendid view over a large stretch of the Arctic Ocean. With the help of the Consul's strong arm I quickly descended, and soon all of us were seated in a clean wooden hut, refreshing ourselves with cream.

Norwegian hospitality and kindness are almost proverbial. While a large spread was being given at the Russian Consul's to all the naval officers and gentlemen of our party, we were asked by Mrs. Holmboe and her daughter to an entertainment, which was held at 1 P.M. Our meal consisted of chocolate and cakes, certainly most delicious. The Norwegians' principal repast is usually served at 4 P.M., following the German custom. The iron stoves that are found in almost every house are terrible pieces of furniture. They are several feet high, and in a very few minutes the room becomes absolutely stifling. Accustomed as English people are to enjoy plenty of fresh air, this close atmosphere made me feel very uncomfortable.

Vardoe is not without a history, for it has been the rendezvous of distinguished arctic explorers, such as Sir Hugh Willoughby, Chancellor, Pet, Barents, so long as three centuries ago; and recently and frequently of Captain Wiggins, and of Dr. Nansen's expedition in search of the North Pole.

At last we began to think of leaving Vardoe. Meantime a fresh stock of provisions had been laid in to satisfy our wants during our arctic expedition. In fact the front part of the ship looked more like a sort of floating farm-yard,—sheep, hens, ducks, and rabbits were to provide us with plenty of fresh food, and a dear little goat was to supply us daily with fresh milk.

On the 22nd August the three Russian steamers, accompanied by the *Minusinsk*, sailed out of the harbour. Anxious to wait for the mail boat, which we hoped might bring us our last good tidings from home, we remained till the following day, when the *Orestes* and *Blencathra* followed the rest of the squadron and put out to sea.

CHAPTER IV

A BRIGHT sunny morning favoured our departure from Vardoe, as the *Blencathra* and *Orestes* weighed anchor and steamed out of the harbour at 4.30 A.M. I was in bed, but from my port-hole anxiously caught a last glimpse of the little island and all its "fishy" attractions. As usual, head-winds and a nasty sea greeted us, and the uncomfortable roll soon found me a ready victim.

A calm smooth sea was afterwards all the more appreciated, as I had learnt from experience that no source of happiness can satisfy our ambitious desires without a previous antithesis of discomfort.

My diary of August the 23rd marks an uneventful day, as we were out of sight of land and it had

turned very cold, stormy, and foggy. I was told
that fogs are very prevalent in those high latitudes
during the summer months, whereas in the winter
the atmosphere is always brilliantly clear.

Next day, on going up on deck, I found the
ship presenting quite an arctic appearance. A
crow's nest had been fastened on to the main
topmast to facilitate a good look-out for ice or
other impediment. The situation fascinated me
enormously, and my wish was to climb to the
top, and had it not been for my petticoat encum-
brances I should not have hesitated to follow in
the sailors' track. The following day the wind
dropped. The diversion we enjoyed during the
morning was exchanging signals with the *Orestes*
by means of the code. I soon learnt the alphabet,
and in fact after a time acquired quite an amount
of nautical knowledge. The crew interested
me ; I liked their company and listening to their
yarns ; I watched all their movements up on deck,
while the hauling of the sails and the sing-song cries
of the men as they pulled away at a rope gave
me ever fresh amusement. Their consideration

for me during the whole of the voyage will remain an enduring feature of my first trip at sea.

In the afternoon we were towed by the *Orestes,*—a delightful sensation. She was going full-speed, and we glided behind with scarcely any perceptible motion. No land was to be seen, all seemed gloom and eternal silence. Kolguiev Island was passed, but being at a considerable distance west of it we were unable to distinguish any outline.

Early dawn on August the 26th disclosed our first wintry scene. A heavy fall of snow was covering the rigging and decks, and on the horizon several blocks of ice began to foreshadow arctic regions, and my wildest expectations seemed about to be thoroughly realised. Towards noon, however, the sun was shining brightly in a cloudless sky, and so pure and clear was the atmosphere that I almost felt as though new life had taken possession of me. Scarcely had we finished our meals when, one and all, we resumed our posts on deck.

The evening was glorious; never have I seen

such magnificent sky effects ; every colour seemed
harmoniously blended.   For a short time we
were able to distinguish the south coast of
Novaia Zemlia, a name so closely associated
with dark schoolroom days, and a place I had
always looked upon as belonging to quite another
world, little thinking that in years to come I
should myself be navigating in the very waters
surrounding it.

On the 27th of August I was on deck at 5.30
A.M., much to the delight of Mr. Popham, whose
grievance at my being so "lazy" was almost daily
expatiated upon.   Certainly there is nothing like
the fresh morning air, but most people are too
fond of cushioned luxury ever to realise the
delights of early dawn, seeming to agree with
Charles Lamb's parody on "Home, Sweet
Home"—

> Be it ever so bedly, there is nothing like bed.

At 7 A.M. we dropped anchor in a sheltered
nook, formed by the island of Waigatz, near the
entrance to the Pet or Yugor Straits, which
separate the island from the mainland almost at

the boundary between Russia proper and Siberia. We found the three Russian vessels lying at anchor, having arrived the previous day, also a Russian man-of-war, called *Nayesdnick*, under the command of Captain Pell, and we greatly wondered what she might be doing in such an outlandish place. We learnt afterwards that she had been ordered there from St. Petersburg for the purpose of supplying Lieutenant Dobrotvorscy with extra fur clothing and provisions for the crews of his ships. She was also to receive despatches from him, and take the opportunity of doing some surveying and watching the Straits; for Norwegian sloops had been caught poaching in Russian waters, and in consequence the Kara Sea was now debarred to them for walrus hunting.

The surrounding scenery was dismal and gloomy in the extreme. Waigatz Island, which stretched to our left, presents a long narrow strip of land, of most sombre uninviting appearance, slightly undulated; the surface is covered with mossy tundras. The island is inhabited by natives called Samoyedes,

with whom, shortly afterwards, we became well
acquainted. They have large herds of reindeer,
which may be seen grazing away. The coast-
line to our right looked none the more inviting.
After breakfast a young Lieutenant from the
Russian man-of-war came on board the *Blencathra* to pay his respects. He was tall, fair,
and promised to be remarkably handsome, and
as he had a certain knowledge of French we
were able to converse with him. He told us
that Dr. Nansen had anchored some time in
this vicinity, and had only left to resume his
polar researches ten days ago. The ice in the
Kara Sea had up to that date formed a slight
impediment to his movements, while in our
case, coming as we did later in the season, it
presented to us no difficulty whatsoever. The
young Lieutenant complained bitterly of the
loneliness and dreariness of the surroundings.
His man-of-war had been anchored for some
time, and certainly there seemed little attraction
for any one, much less for youthful flightiness.
Through the narrow passage of the Straits de-

tached ice-floes kept drifting by in all sorts of grotesque shapes.

Anxiously curious to have a look at the ice in the Kara Sea, and to judge for ourselves the real and exact condition of what we were to expect, we resolved to steam through in the *Blencathra*. Being of wood, she feared no shock, even had we laid ourselves open to any such risk, consequently we weighed anchor and set forth. The opening to the Straits is very narrow, scarcely exceeding three miles in width. The scenery continued to assume characteristically arctic appearances. Drift ice was encountered to a large extent, but of a soft and harmless nature, and, as far as we could judge, future prospects looked very promising. Elated with the good tidings, we returned to our anchorage, a favourable signal flying at the topmast for the benefit of all our companions, but it was very cold and the sea was uncomfortably rough.

On August the 28th the arrival of the *Minusinsk* greatly reduced our anxiety, for

no one had come across her since leaving Vardoe. However, all had gone well. I spent
part of the day busily writing letters, not that
I had so much to relate, but the fact of heading them with the word " Siberia " sounded
so grand and uncommon that I gave a free rein
to my imagination.

In the afternoon we paid a return call on
board the Russian man - of - war. The captain
and officers received us in the most hospitable
manner, champagne flowing liberally and numerous toasts being drunk to our good luck and
success. After entrusting our letters to one of
the officers, we bade farewell and returned on
board the *Blencathra*. The waves meanwhile
had been lashed to fury, and I felt somewhat
frightened in the small steam-launch, but found
no sympathy whatsoever from my friends, who
were rather amused than otherwise at my alarm.
The weather all this time had been too unfavourable to allow of our indulging in a stroll ashore.

At early dawn on the 29th August our little
fleet weighed anchor and steamed cautiously

through the Straits. The morning was bright
but damp. I was up on deck at 6 A.M., and
two hours later we sighted the small hamlet
of Khabarova, where we anchored a short time.
It is situated on the sandy beach, and consists
of wooden houses and Samoyede tents clustering
round a little wooden church recently erected
by a wealthy Siberian, Mr. Siberiakoff. Our
object in dropping anchor off this quaint settlement was to land Mr. Jackson and his retinue
among the natives. Two boat-loads of Samoyedes,—men, women, and children, rowed meanwhile towards the *Orestes* to wish Captain Wiggins
a hearty welcome. During his many successful
trips to the Yenesei River, Captain Wiggins
had formed great friendships with the natives,
and his kindly expression and unaffected manner
had won him a well-deserved popularity. They
were, one and all, delighted to see him, and
clambered up on board the *Orestes* as fast as
they could; it was quite touching to witness
the meeting.

Before proceeding any further a slight intro-

duction to the Samoyedes will perhaps be
of interest. They inhabit a large tract of
country, stretching from Archangel to the Yenesei
River, and are numbered among the human
family under the head of Hyperborean Mon-
golidæ. By imperial decree they are freed from
military service, territorial contributions, and from
taxes in money, only having to pay in skins of
wild beasts captured by them. The Samoyedes
are very diminutive and broad shouldered, have
round flat faces of yellowish colour, prominent
cheek-bones, tiny black eyes, small open nose,
thick lips, very little beard, and long coarse black
hair. In constitution they are weak and get prematurely old. Their morals are extremely simple,
and in manners they are good tempered. The
Samoyedes pass the summer near the rivers and
lakes, occupied in fishing; at the approach
of spring they migrate to near the sea,
trading in marine animals. Wandering from
the sea, they disperse over the tundra for
the capture of bears, foxes, white foxes, ermines,
and squirrels. Although the Samoyedes by

such kind of occupation belong to the hunting people, yet their prosperity lies in the pasturage of reindeer.

The Samoyedes never remain long in one place, but wander about in search of fresh food for their reindeer. In such a mode of life there is not, nor can there be, any fixed habitation, but the natives live in the so-called *tchoom* or tent, for the construction of which they fix.some poles in the ground and cover them with reindeer skins, so that by such an enclosure the dwelling of the Samoyede has the form of a cone. In the middle of the tchoom is a plate of iron, or a kind of stone, in which they cook their food. The tchoom is extremely dirty inside, and the air most unsavoury. The Samoyedes' dress in winter or summer is always the same, and is formed of reindeer skins. They wear a sort of long tunic, called *sovik*, having an opening to put the head through ; the hair of the garment is worn outside in fine weather and inside when it rains. A pair of short drawers made of reindeer skin, tight round the hips and reaching downward to the knee, stockings of peshki (the

skin of young fawns) with the hair inwards, and
boots, called *poumé leepté*, of strong reindeer hide,
complete the costume. Their garments are
singularly well adapted to the wants of the inhabitants in these rigorous climes. The Samoyedes
wear a girdle round the loins, beautifully beaded,
from which is suspended a knife.

The garments of the fair sex are adorned
with various coloured skins, among which a piece
of European-coloured cloth is found frequently
inserted. They seem very vain, particularly of
their hair, which hangs in a long tight plait
down the back, ornamented with all sorts of pieces
of metal, giving them a most ludicrous appearance. Indeed they seem to pick up every kind
of brass and iron fragments, which make quite a
chink when they move.

The Samoyedes live chiefly on reindeer flesh,
and consider the blood of this animal a delicate
and wholesome drink. Besides this, they eat
wolves, bears, foxes, etc., as well as fish and
birds. As regards intelligence, the Samoyedes up
to the present live in extreme ignorance; they

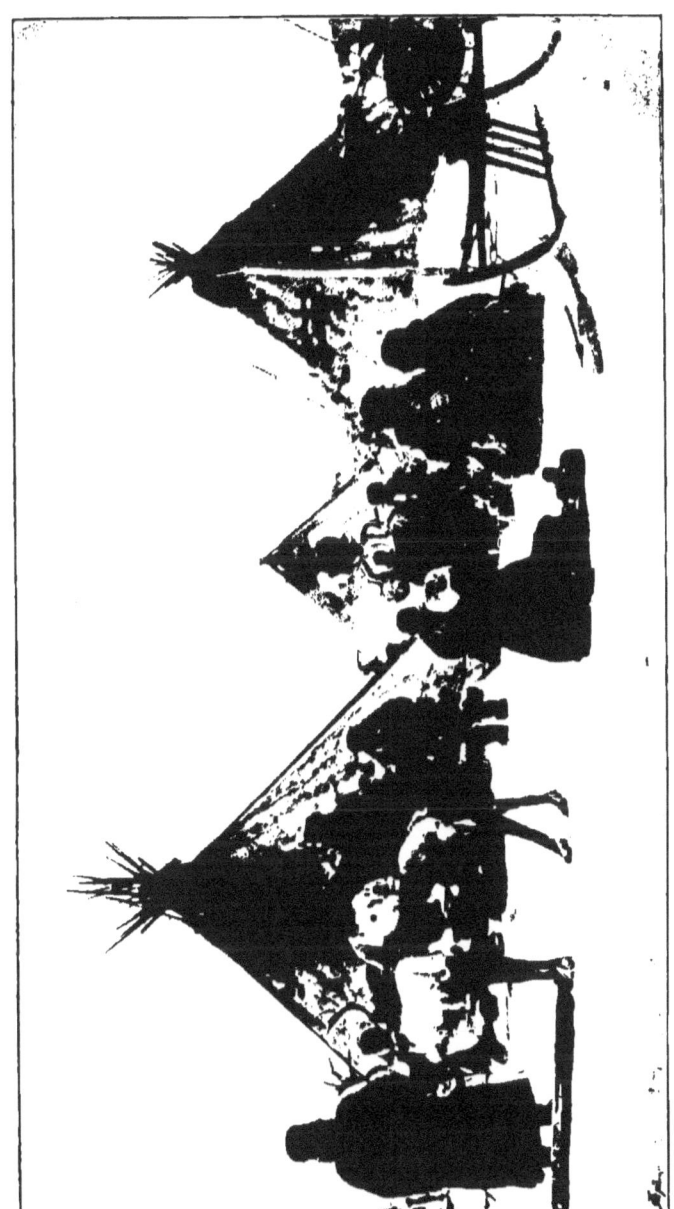

A SAMOYEDE SETTLEMENT.

To face page 40.

cannot count time, are illiterate, and, like all
nomad tribes, inclined to drunkenness. The
greater number are of the Greek Orthodox
Church, having been converted by Russian priests
who visit their localities. Several of them, however, still continue to worship idols in the shape
of dolls, and perform their heathen ceremonies
through the medium of "Shamans" or medicine
men. The name Samoyede is said to occur in
Russian chronicles as far back as the year 1096,
and means salmon-eaters.

We were all anxious to go on shore and stand
on Siberian soil. Steam was got up in the small
launch, and after breakfast we landed at Khabarova, where all the inhabitants had collected on
the beach to see us. A very inharmonious chorus
of dogs replied to our greeting, whose boisterous
welcome their masters had difficulty in sup-
pressing. Our reception was most friendly;
they shook hands in a most cordial manner, and,
notwithstanding their somewhat repulsive appearance, particularly in the case of the women, one
could not help taking a lively interest in their

condition. Among them were several Russian traders from the Petchora, who during the short summer months trade in European goods in exchange for furs, skins, etc.

The people showed us their tents, reindeer, and sledges, and took us over the wooden house where their priest resided. His countenance did not please me, for he had rather a sinister look, with long hair hanging in curls on his shoulders. I was told that he was so addicted to drunkenness that he was obliged to be strapped on to his bed on account of his violence. Civilisation is certainly a beneficent acquisition to the human family, not unmixed, however, in its earlier stages of development, with consequences which time alone can remedy. Russian sloops coming to trade from the Petchora have barrels of vodka and spirits on board, which the Samoyedes sacrifice much to acquire, in order to satisfy their craving for the newly-introduced stimulant.

A Russian merchant, a tall handsome man in Samoyede dress, with a cap of reindeer skin, the strings of which were ornamented by pieces of cloth, offered to take me for a drive in his sledge, drawn by six reindeer. I immediately accepted his kind offer, seating myself on the narrow seat beside him. He carried a long prong instead of a whip, and no sooner were we ready to start than the reindeer, all harnessed abreast, began to pull and gallop at full speed. No snow was then covering the ground, so, heedless of obstacles, we bumped and jolted in the most fearful manner, so much so that to prevent being thrown off the sledge I had to cling with both my arms round my companion's neck. The soil was very marshy and undulating, but nothing seemed to slacken the speed of the reindeer, so I shouted at the top of my voice, in response to which the Russian kept soothing me in terms unfortunately unknown to me. This drive was unique, and I am sure few people can boast of a similar experience. On returning, another prepossessing Russian seemed anxious to sledge with me, and as it was difficult to resist his pressing invitation, I set off on a second trial. It certainly was a case of admiration conquering fear.

Meantime Mr. Jackson was busy landing his belongings and provisions, which were to last him several months. He took up his abode in the priest's house, and his room, adjoining the priest's, seemed comfortable enough, although with only the bare necessaries of life. After seeing him settled down among the Samoyedes, without the slightest knowledge of their language and without a friend, we left him our blessing and bade him farewell. On parting, my Russian merchant presented me with a young fox, which unfortunately died on the voyage.

We were now about to enter the Kara or Black Sea, nicknamed by the Russian academician Von Baer,—the great " Ice-cellar."

CHAPTER V

ON the 29th of August at 1 P.M. we were again under way. The *Blencathra* took the lead, followed in her wake by the *Orestes* and the *Minusinsk*, the three Russian vessels bringing up the rear.

In the afternoon we entered the Kara Sea, which was to me full of interest. First of all, the fact that I was the first lady who had navigated its waters naturally caused me great delight ; secondly, it had been pictured to me before my departure with every sort of danger, a warning which appeared all the more to entice me. Far from being seized with a sudden longing for familiar surroundings and home - like scenery, this arctic aspect seemed to produce so great a fascination upon me as to be almost unaccountable. No one has any idea of the glories revealed day after day in those high and, comparatively speaking, almost unknown latitudes. I had often been told that when explorers once direct their steps northwards they get bitten with the desire of returning again and again; and now I can speak for myself, and strongly endorse this statement. Our navigation through the Kara Sea was perfectly delightful. In fact so clear and placid was the water that I felt as if I had suddenly been transferred to the Lake of Geneva, and our passage through this northern sea recalled to my mind the many pleasant yachting expeditions I have enjoyed on those beautiful southern waters.

The entrance to the Kara Sea presented a most mystic and arctic appearance. Ice-fields, low and comparatively level, were to be seen floating towards the Straits, while ice-floes and icebergs formed a striking feature in the picturesque aspect of the sea. They were of a bluish-

ICE-FLOES.

green tint, and as the sun was shining, the bright light displayed wonderful beauty of form and brilliancy. They assume every variety of colour and prismatic appearance. Sometimes the top is table-shaped with acute cones, with numerous clefts and rents, giving the appearance of many distinct spires. On the other hand they display vast hollows or caverns, occasionally perforated. In fact the diversity of form and structure is so endless, as to defy altogether my powers of description.

I shall never forget the effect produced upon me as I stood up on deck and gazed with silent delight on the splendid and impressive panorama. The silence was alone broken by the motion of our little fleet. It kept meandering and dodging the ice with skilful precision. No land was visible. A deathly stillness was unbroken by the slightest sound, and an oppressive loneliness seemed to weigh upon one. But not so on board the *Blencathra*. A more joyful gathering it would be impossible to find, surrounded as we were by all the luxuries which enhance the recreations of life. It was difficult to imagine that we were not in the very midst of civilisation, but steaming pleasantly on the waters of the much dreaded Kara Sea.

Every question put to me on arrival in England to the effect, "Was it not dreadfully cold?" received a decided negative answer. The sun shone brightly, not a cloud intercepted our view of the great vault of heaven, and so mild was the atmosphere that we slept all night with open port-holes, feeling all the better for it. My costume, which in fact formed my daily and never-varying dress throughout the whole of the voyage, may be summed up in very few words. A blue serge skirt, jacket to match, which by the way was not lined, a red flannel shirt, and a straw sailor-hat, constituted my seafaring habiliment. Very slight addition to my usual underclothing was made, and, I may honestly add, that I scarcely suffered from the effects of the cold. In the excitement of my departure from England I had omitted to provide myself with any furs whatsoever, much to the surprise of the Russian officers, who laughed at seeing me thus equipped, and suggested that my attire was far better adapted for the soft summer breezes of the Mediterranean.

Dulness never once reigned among us ; that was a quality we none of us possessed. The mind was constantly occupied with fresh scenes and the anticipation of new and varied excitements. Most of our days were spent up on deck. When, however, we were obliged to seek refuge in the main cabin, every variety of occupation attended us. Musical instruments were a source of great delight. Mr. Popham was particularly well gifted, and gave full vent to his talent on the violin, whilst I accompanied him on the piano and Mr. James added to the chorus his skilful performance on the flute, Mrs. James meanwhile constituting our sole but competent and appreciative critic. Often also the rolls attached to the organum were worked by Mr. Popham, who, while playing the violin, made use of his legs to blow the windpipes. Our evenings were thus delightfully spent, and hours sped with such rapidity that the clock almost always struck twelve before we thought of retiring.

Books were also much appreciated. Mr. Popham generally read to us aloud, and I meanwhile worked at comforters and petticoats for the poor in England.

As we steamed along the ice gradually disappeared. On the 30th of August we sighted the bleak and desolate looking coast line of the Yalmal Peninsula, in latitude 72°. The weather was lovely, the sea perfectly smooth. Towards evening the Russian paddle-steamer parted company, having received orders to inspect the narrow Strait which separates White Island from the mainland. These Straits were found to be in the same shallow and dangerous condition as when surveyed by Captain Wiggins in 1874-76-78, useless for navigation, with tortuous channels, boisterous currents, and shoals all round.

Great excitement prevailed one evening while we were at dinner. The skipper came to inform us that on two ice-floes 200 walruses were to be seen lying huddled together. A tremendous commotion reigned among the crew. Each man that could be spared stood on the prow,

armed with a gun. We steamed quietly towards
the first ice-floe; when comparatively close a
regular fusilade from the guns was followed by
the plunge of all the walrus into the water, roaring
and bellowing, and much infuriated at being thus
molested. Disappointed at our failure, we resolved to approach more cautiously the next ice-
floe, where lay as many walrus as on the first one.
Accordingly an order was given that no shots
were to be fired. Mr. Popham, however, had the
dinghy lowered, then sprang into it armed with a
gun and rowed off towards the scene of action.
The great art in striking the animal a fatal blow is
to shoot it in the nape of the neck, death being the
instantaneous result. The walrus, however, were
not to be tampered with. They raised their heads,
and upon seeing the enemy plunged, one and all,
into the water. The small boat was instantly surrounded by dozens of huge beasts, but Mr. Popham,
with the cool calm manner and careless intrepidity
so characteristic of him, showed no fear of the
impending danger. On the other hand we
thought every moment that these fierce sea-lions,

enraged almost to madness, would make a dash for him. Naturally we looked on in breathless emotion. Such a scene can never be forgotten. Mr. Popham kept firing to keep them off, nearly deafened by their roaring, as they dived and rose, looking fiercely at him. So skilful was he that he managed to kill a large female walrus and her young one, which by natural instinct had been following its mother. Both were seized, towed and hauled on to an ice-floe ; and our excitement reached its zenith. The skinning process then took place. The hide and blubber were taken off, and the head was severed from the body to form a trophy of sporting prowess and peril escaped. Leaving the carcasses behind, we set sail. It had become very late, 11 P.M., but shortly afterwards we had rejoined our fleet.

The most remarkable point in the walrus is the great length of two of its upper teeth, which extend downwards for nearly two feet. These tusks are used by the walrus for climbing the rocks or heaps of ice, and also for digging up the seaweed, on which the animal mostly subsists. The length of the walrus is about sixteen feet, but its head is very small in proportion. The expression of its countenance is very ferocious, principally on account of the enormous size of the upper lip and the thick bristles with which it is covered. Naturally the walrus is often hunted for the sake of its flesh, its oil, its skin, and its teeth ; but their skin is so strong and slippery that even a sharp weapon frequently glides off without injuring the animal. The great enemy of the walrus is the polar bear, but against this foe he is said to defend himself most vigorously with his tusks.

After coasting along the Yalmal Peninsula we rounded White Island, and soon were out of sight of land again. By the 1st of September we had reached our most northerly point, being as far north as latitude 74°, only 16 degrees from the North Pole. I felt so excited at being comparatively in such close vicinity to the pole, that had we suddenly turned our prow northwards and changed our goal, the spirit of enterprise and adventure would have taken full possession

of me. The brown colour of the water denoted
that we were steaming abreast of the estuary of
the River Obi, and shortly afterwards a wintry
scene again disclosed itself. It had turned decidedly colder, and next day the deck and rigging
were covered with snow and icicles. Again we
met with ice-fields and ice-floes, which necessi-
tated careful steering. Sparkling under a blue
sky and brilliant sunshine, the ice formed a *coup
d'œil* as striking as it was beautiful. It struck
me as curious that ice abounded in great quantity
at the entrance to the Pet Straits and between
the estuaries of the Obi and Yenesei Rivers, with
open water the whole distance between the two
boundaries just mentioned, and presenting no
difficulty whatsoever for navigation. In fact, I
was on the whole rather disappointed with the
Kara Sea, as everything was far too plain sailing ; no adventures occurred on the way, and
nothing even to cause the slightest anxiety. I
began to realise the fact that after all one can
never depend on other people's reports, but to
go and see for one's self is the best solution to

any doubt. At the same time I may add, without hesitation, that I thoroughly enjoyed my cruise through the Kara Sea—the passage was glorious, the floating ice met with proved no insuperable barrier, as we were led to believe it would, and so calm was the sea that our swing table was fixed all the way from the Pet Straits.

Apart from seeing walrus, which we did in large numbers, we also perceived several seals and wild duck, which our friends occasionally fired at for the sake of sport. I fancied I saw a polar bear in the distance, but unfortunately we came into no close contact with this formidable antagonist.

On the 2nd of September we sighted Port Dickson and entered the mouth of the mighty Yenesei River, which at its estuary expands like a lake, with a breadth of forty miles, interspersed with islands. The river had hitherto been but little navigated, consequently we possessed no charts, and our compasses being imperfect, we had to rely entirely on Captain Wiggins' experience and knowledge, gathered from previous voyages. The lead was kept going, showing a depth varying from seven to four fathoms. Some slight anxiety was attached to the *Orestes*, for had she gone aground, carrying 1600 tons of rails, the consequences might have been serious. Captain Wiggins' characteristic caution, however, allayed all apprehension.

We were coasting comfortably along the left bank at a rate of four knots. The familiar flat dreary coast here again met our eyes, only slightly varied by white patches of snow. We were beginning to grow weary of such slow locomotion, and were longing to drop anchor at our destination. At last in the distance, on the right-hand side, several lights gleamed through the darkness, indicating a recognition of our arrival. The Russian screw and schooner were already lying at anchor, and the River Expedition, under the command of Lieutenant Zalyeffsky, was there to receive us. We met with a most enthusiastic and cordial reception—guns were repeatedly fired, rockets rent the air, and Bengal lights illuminated fantastically the weird scenery. We had successfully reached Golchika in latitude 71° 40″ N., dropping anchor on the 3rd of September at 10.30 P.M., having accomplished a distance of some 3000 miles.

The evening was beautiful; a bright moon was shining in a clear sky, which seemed to add colouring to our much elated spirits. We were delighted with our successful enterprise, and did full justice to the occasion by, to use an amusing phrase, "thoroughly wetting our luck."

A short summary of some of the noteworthy voyages in or across the Kara Sea may interest my readers. Unfortunately not all attempts to penetrate the great "Ice-cellar" have been successful. The very first effort that was ever made by Western Europeans was by our countryman Sir Hugh Willoughby in 1553. It ended disastrously. He was followed forty-five years later by the brave Dutch Captain Barents, who was obliged to winter on the east coast of Novaia Zemlia, his ship having been ice-bound, and he eventually died of scurvy. The Austro-Hungarian Expedition also met with an unfortunate result.

Notwithstanding these failures, two names

stand pre-eminently forward coupled with remarkable successes. Every person having adequate interest in arctic expeditions has heard of
Captain Joseph Wiggins, so thoroughly associated
as his name has been with the records of Kara Sea
navigation, of which indeed he may be said to
be the original promoter, thereby opening a
new highway over these waters for the service
of commercial enterprise amongst nations, and
general benefit is certain to proceed from the intercourse thus created. His voyages are adequate
testimony to his knowledge and experience of
the Siberian sea route. His first venturesome
attempt to navigate these waters was made in
1874. He entered the Kara Sea as early as
June 24th, by way of the Kara Straits, in the
Diana, and cruised about in that sea for eight
weeks. His subsequent voyages in the *Thames*,
Warkworth, Phœnix, Labrador, Orestes, etc.,
sufficiently establish the reputation of Captain
Wiggins as a great navigator and as an enthusiastic and successful explorer. He has won by
his kindly manner and extreme modesty the love

and admiration of all who know him. Indeed I feel proud in being able to number myself among his many friends and appreciative admirers.

Another name which deserves special mention is that of Professor Nordenskiöld, the distinguished Swedish naturalist. He followed in Captain Wiggins' track, entering the Kara Sea in 1875 in the *Proeven*, and proceeding to the mouth of the Yenesei River, doing likewise the following year in the *Ymer*. These voyages ultimately led to Professor Nordenskiöld's celebrated journey through the Behring Straits round the whole north of Siberia on board the *Vega* in 1878.

The Kara Sea may be said to have been for several years the happy hunting-ground of Norwegian walrus-hunters.

Dr. Nansen also, in furtherance of his expedition towards the North Pole, recently passed across the Kara Sea ; and in conclusion let us hope that his aim and anticipation will meet with success outshining that of all previous expeditions, and that he may rank as the greatest arctic explorer the world has ever produced.

F

CHAPTER VI

NEXT morning we were all on deck early.
Nothing, however, rewarded our eager gaze.
A dull barren coast-line was alone distinguish-
able, and a few wooden houses and reindeer
tents constituted the small village of Golchika.
Situated on an island at the mouth of a small
tributary stream on the right bank of the Yenesei,
it lies at a distance of 200 miles up the river.

The weather was anything but pleasant. A
strong west wind was blowing, and we experienced
continual snowstorms during the day. In the
course of the afternoon we went ashore, landing
in a small creek, and on the shore were numerous

Siberian convicts and prisoners, sent down the river in lighters to help in the trans-shipment of the rails from on board the *Orestes.* They certainly did not excite any commiseration, for they looked quite happy and contented, as if they rather enjoyed the "spree."

We next directed our steps towards the habitations, escorted by the Priest of Turukhansk. He was robed in long flowing black garments; his hair with serpentine curls encircled his shoulders. He had a sly look about him, with a rollicking jovial expression, and was as active as a kitten. On reaching a wooden hut, which was the largest of the group, we stepped in to have a look at the inmates. On opening the door a pestilential mephitic atmosphere burst upon us. In fact the odour of the Samoyede is peculiar to himself, and so sickening and overpowering that it quite beggars description.

However we entered, and I feel justified in saying that no less than two dozen human beings, men, women, and children, were to be seen lying indiscriminately huddled together.

The heat was oppressive, and the air thick with smoke. It was difficult to distinguish anything. I nevertheless perceived that these Samoyedes, familiar objects since our contact with them at Khabarova, or St. Nicholai, as it is now named, were very slightly clad. The children went barefooted and barelegged, with merely a transparent loose cotton princess dress down to the knees. The women were not better off in that respect. But these uncivilised customs are not without reason. Born and bred in such remote parts, where scarcely any stranger up to the present has ever passed their threshold, they have to make the best of their existence, and depend on the result of their hunting for clothing. When they leave their huts to imbibe a little fresh air they put on the thickest fur garments they can provide, and so hardly feel the difference of temperature when they go out to face the cold. Once home again they promptly divest themselves of them.

The Samoyedes, whose type is the same as those described at Khabarova, seemed delighted to welcome us. We of course could not converse with them, but our pantomimic efforts seemed to produce the same effect as speech, and they responded likewise. Never having seen European ladies before, their curiosity was very much aroused by our appearance, dress, and physique. They even ventured to touch my blue serge skirt and jacket, and wondered what it might be made of. But what tickled their fancy more than anything else was a diamond buckle which I wore on my belt, and a sparkling brooch. They seemed in raptures over them. I could see their admiring eyes intently fixed upon them, as they are very fond of anything that shines or glitters. Our respective relationships seemed to puzzle them also very much. The skipper happened to be standing behind me, and I suppose he impressed them with a certain air of paternity, so I was put down as his daughter. It was most entertaining, as my new acquaintances continued to indulge in many varied conjectures regarding me and my companions, and these blunders were a source of great amusement, for I fairly went

through several imaginary phases. The Samoyedes appeared to be much pitted with small-pox,
and altogether looked rather unhealthy. As a
preventive against scurvy they dip the food they
eat into the reindeer's blood, which is supposed
to act as an antidote.

Next to the room where all the natives were
huddled together was a very clean nice-looking
chamber inhabited by a priest. It looked very
comfortable, with the inevitable "ikon" or sacred
picture hanging up in a corner. We were obliged
to sit down for a few minutes, and he offered us
some refreshments, which, however, we declined.

Golchika seemed infested with Eskimo dogs,
most of them being white and very much like
wolves, and from time to time setting up inharmonious wolfish howls. One of them was extremely handsome, and Mr. Popham having
expressed a wish to possess one was presented
with it before leaving.

The three weeks anchored off Golchika were
neither very eventful nor interesting. We experienced very nasty gales almost all the time, and

very rarely could we go ashore. We, however, wiled away the time by eating, drinking, reading, playing, and sleeping, cooped up as we were from morning to night in the main cabin. Notwithstanding the dreariness of the situation, a slight coating of snow varying the monotone gray of the coast-line, I never felt dull. Perhaps it was the anticipation of excitement and adventure which kept me in spirits.

Meanwhile, when the river was calm, the *Orestes* was busy discharging her rails on to the lighters. The *Minusinsk* was also getting ready to go as soon as posssible up the river to Yeneseisk, to take despatches and letters for the Russian Government. No news could have been received of our little fleet since our leaving the Pet Straits, and the much dreaded Kara Sea was sure to cause a certain amount of anxiety.

The sameness of our daily routine was broken one day by the announcement of our projected intention of all going up the river to Yeneseisk and sleighing home *viâ* Krasnoiarsk, Tobolsk, Tiumen, Moscow, and St. Petersburg.

This sudden change in our programme naturally caused a considerable ebullition of spirits, and for several days filled us with the hope of entering the very heart of Siberia. We kept discussing suggested changes and making endless arrangements to carry out the project. We even went on board the Russian river paddle-steamer to secure accommodation, which was nice though rather primitive. However all this fell through after a time, much to my disappointment. I was longing to see more of Siberian life and people, and something of Russia and all her interesting inhabitants. Life is said to be made up of one long string of disappointments, so I cheerfully acquiesced in my fate, and should advise all my readers to do likewise under similar circumstances.

Taking advantage of a fine day, we rowed ashore to take a walk over the tundra. On landing up the creek we found the ground extremely swampy, and had it not been for some excellent galoshes purchased at Vardoe, I should have fared very ill. We found a sledge, to which were harnessed five reindeer—splendid animals, waiting

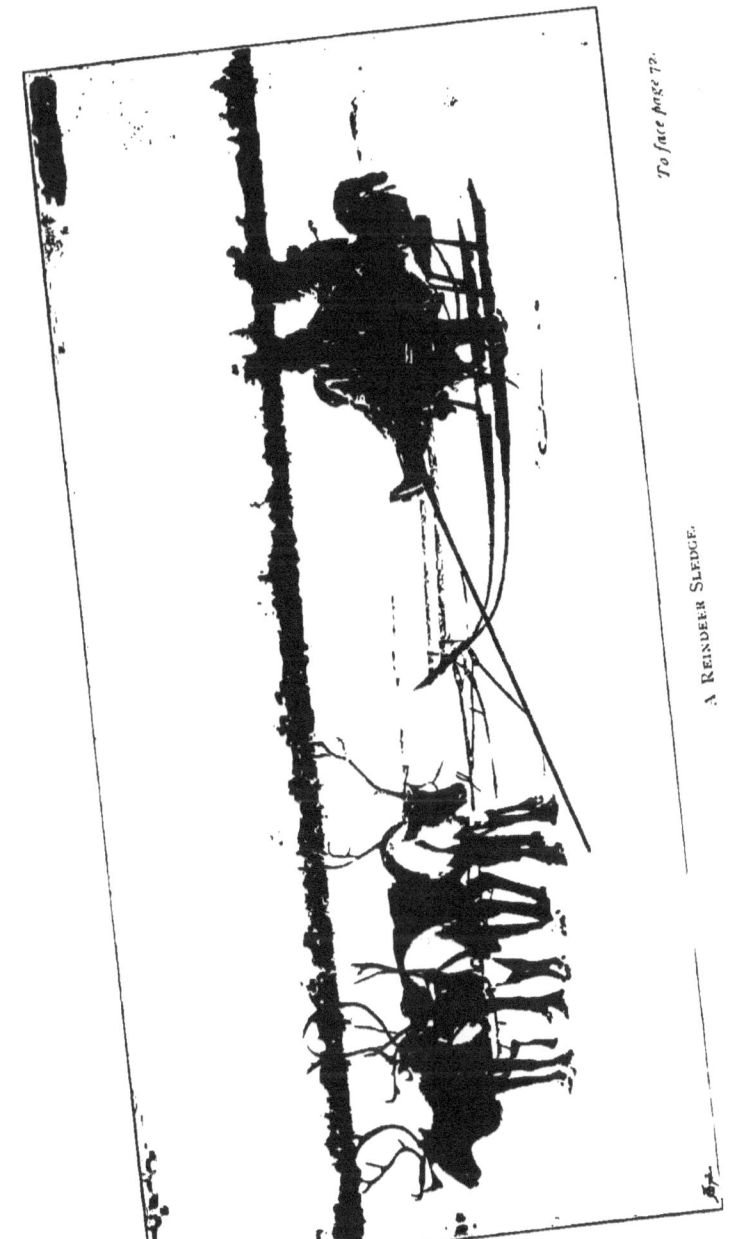

To face page 72.

A REINDEER SLEDGE.

with extreme patience. They are about four feet in height, and perhaps four to five feet in length, with huge branching antlers, covered at this period of the year with soft velvet. The colour of those we saw was mostly white, tinged with brown all down the back. They are strong powerful animals, but looked very gentle and good-natured. When alive the animal draws the sledge, and when dead its flesh is eaten and the skin used for tent and clothing.

One of the reindeer attached to the sledge which we saw, looked lame, and was soon condemned as unfit for service. A Samoyede and his wife shortly afterwards appeared on the scene and began to remove the fine reindeer from the others. Thinking they were only going to pat it and take it home, I followed them to see the result, but to my horror and amazement the uncanny old Samoyede produced a hatchet, and, striking the animal a severe blow on the head, felled it in a moment. Turning the reindeer over, he plunged a knife behind the shoulder into the heart, in order to allow the blood to flow straight into the stomach, and not saturate the whole body, thus in a very few seconds putting an end to this graceful animal. It made a great impression upon me, and yet I could not tear myself away from the scene. I learnt afterwards that this sudden act of butchery was owing to the old Samoyede wanting to gain a little money from our fleet in exchange for a leg or shoulder of reindeer.

After this we proceeded on our stroll and came across several curious-looking objects dotted about. On approaching we found them to be wooden sledges, covered up with furs. My curiosity led me to make a nearer inspection. To my horror I found that these sledges formed the burial-place of the Samoyedes. The dead bodies are thus placed on them, covered with their furs, and left exposed. On removing the rug I also perceived the decayed carcass of a dog lying next to the corpse. I was told that it was the Samoyede custom to kill a favourite Eskimo dog whenever a death occurs. We met with many of these burial-places, some quite tiny sledges, containing babies, others apparently empty, with only bones strewn round about. I suspect wild animals are often to be seen prowling around.

The weather was nice and bright, but before we had time to return a snowstorm overtook us. In rowing back to the *Blencathra* such nasty choppy waves arose that I was alarmed, and on our way home we stopped and called on the Russian officers on board the schooner. Their kind hospitality once again made itself felt, and only after we had partaken of wine and various refreshments were we allowed to depart. Although I never indulge in spirits of any kind, I could not refuse what was offered, as a token of good-will, and as it gave me the chance of raising a glass to the happiness and well-being of our kind friends.

The next day, September the 11th, was the Czar's birthday, and it was similarly acknowledged and celebrated with due honour and respect. The weather was glorious, a brilliant sunshine illuminating the weird scenery. Salutes were repeatedly fired, and our combined fleets were bedecked with flags, looking extremely bright. I could hardly believe that I was some 3000 miles distant from England, several hundreds of miles from civilisation, and only about 19 degrees from the North Pole. Yet there I was, body and soul, in the very heart of the mighty Yenesei River. In the afternoon of the same day the *Minusinsk* left for Yeneseisk, a town situated 1500 miles up the river. She was under the command of Robert Wiggins, brother to the eminent navigator, and, as it turned out, successfully reached her destination on October the 13th, having accomplished the distance in thirty-three days.

On the 13th of September a strong gale of wind sprang up, lasting with extreme violence several days. Although at anchor the motion was most disagreeable.

Two of the Russian barges, which had just been loaded with a cargo of rails, unfortunately met with a disaster.

As no assistance could be given, they began to sink rapidly, much to our distress. No lives, however, were lost. The lighters seemed unfit to carry such a weight, especially under unexpected circumstances, such as this hurricane. The barometer had stood at 29.40, but very shortly afterwards had fallen as low as 28.80, a fall which, according to the skipper, was not to be looked upon with indifference.

Great excitement prevailed when the news spread that the Russian vessels were beginning to drag their anchors, and as we were all anchored more or less close together, we feared a collision. However, what might have proved unpleasant was luckily averted. The Russian vessels battled heroically with the waves, and the officers, deeming it advisable to make for the opposite shore, steamed across to seek shelter.

Next morning we were likewise to meet with the same fate. Our anchors began to drag, and as the sandy bank extended to some considerable distance from the shore, the result might have caused some damage to the yacht. At an early hour the noise of the sailors up on deck awakened in me some suspicion. Hearing the gale howling, the waves lashing in fury, and sharp orders being given, I began to realise what was going on, and very soon afterwards a familiar voice came to warn me to get up and dress, in case of any mishap.

Throwing a glance out of the port-hole, the very look of that nasty cold sea sent shivers down my back. Instead of dwelling on any means of escape, I merely heaped all the cloaks I could find on my bed, and, diving under the bedclothes, I calmly awaited events. My idea was, that if I were to die or drown, why not do so comfortably.

Fully twenty minutes elapsed before I dared uncover my head to listen to what might be going on, when, on doing so, I found everything peaceful and the yacht anchored off the opposite coast. Skilful manœuvring had dispelled all fear of impending danger. Alone the *Orestes* resisted the waves, nobly withstanding their attacks, and only from desire to keep company did she follow in our wake. It seemed hardly credible that one could expect to witness such dreadful gales on a river which, on this occasion so treacherous, at other times smooth and still as a looking‑glass, had won our trust and confidence.

But very often, as in other cases, appearances are deceptive, for I expect that, being so near the wide expanse, which extends to a breadth of forty miles, it was almost like being in open sea, and the wind veering round the corner burst as it were upon us in all its fury.

Lying at anchor, opposite Golchika, we enjoyed considerable shelter, and the *Orestes* was able to continue the trans-shipment of the rails, which was actively carried on. Several Samoyede tents were to be seen clustering near the beach.

We were longing, after so many days of seclusion, to stretch our contracted limbs again, and to make acquaintance with the inhabitants on the left bank. A lovely bright day favoured our intentions. On September the 18th the gentlemen, armed with guns, and the ladies accompanying them, we all set forth, imbued with interest and curiosity, for a day's sport. On landing we were greeted by a whole tribe of

Samoyede women, children, and dogs. The men were out fishing. We laughed and joked, and soon were on familiar terms by means of signs.

They asked us into their tents, which are entirely made up of reindeer skins. In the roof is an aperture for the smoke to escape. On either side were wooden benches, covered with furs, shared by two families. The smell was dreadful, and I could almost see the walls alive with vermin. In fact I was told that almost every night, on divesting themselves of their clothes, the Samoyedes make a regular search and hunt after repulsive insects. I was so terrified at the possibility of their imparting these favourites to me that I kept somewhat at a respectful distance. Shortly afterwards the men appeared on the scene and chimed in most amicably. We gave them some tobacco, of which they are inordinately fond.

Meanwhile we had sent for provisions from the *Blencathra*. Their gratitude, on seeing any amount of tea, sugar, fancy biscuits, wine, etc., was inexpressible, especially when, after a time, they began to realise our friendly intentions.

It struck me very much to see the old Samoyede, apparently chief of the little colony, instantly producing several roubles as recompense for our gift, no doubt the money he had just received for his reindeer from the Russians. We, however, declined his offer. Instead Mr. James carried off a sledge as a curiosity, and Mr. Popham a small Siberian dog, an act they seemed fully to endorse. The port wine produced a most amusing effect. Before we had time to offer any assistance they had broken the neck of the bottle, and spilling half the contents on the ground, poured it out into a sort of wooden bowl. This they all sipped in turns, highly delighted, the result being that their spirits were greatly raised.

At the close of these comical proceedings we began to move over the mosses of the tundras in search of sport. Here also the ground was extremely marshy, with a stretch of country gloomy and uninviting, to which the lack of

G

trees gave a peculiar air of desolation. We had walked but a short distance when we came upon quite a flock of apparently white birds. Our approach did not seem to frighten them in the slightest degree. The gentlemen waited for a favourable moment, and, on firing, several fell victims to the guns. The birds proved to be ptarmigan, splendid game, and just losing the last of their pretty brown plumage in anticipation of winter. The whole afternoon we kept pursuing them, which presented no difficulty, as, unaccustomed to being molested, they were quite tame and fearless. Eventually we returned on board, with a full bag of ptarmigan. We feasted on them for several days. The flavour was most delicate and delicious, to my taste greatly exceeding our grouse in quality. In Siberian they are termed " Rabschish."

I here take occasion, by way of parenthesis, to mention with highest commendation the excellent capabilities of James' patent folding canvas boat. Much was the pleasure and advantage we derived throughout our voyage from its use. The wonderful little skiff was always ready at a moment's notice to convey us through still or stormy waters to visit the shore. Diminutive in size and light in weight, only two seconds were required to get it ready for sea, and yet so strong was it that no feeling of insecurity was entertained as we committed ourselves to its apparently fragile structure. Frequently four persons of our company, no feather-weights either, desirous of going ashore without appealing to any of the crew for aid, and accompanied by several dogs, availed themselves of this handy and trustworthy little vessel. To any ocean-loving adventurer therefore, whom it may concern, and who may happen to read these lines, I strongly recommend James' folding canvas boat.

Later in the afternoon some of the Samoyedes came on board to return our visit. The women looked very smart in their fur cloaks, made up of small bits of various skins, inserted and ornamented with coloured pieces of cloth. They seemed so proud, and kept showing themselves off, greatly rejoicing in our admiration of them ;

and I am sure they were quite unable to take in all they witnessed on board the *Blencathra*, for they looked amazed. It was with quite a feeling of regret that we bade them good-bye. For a moment I tried to imagine myself in their position, left alone during the terrible long arctic winter, away from civilisation and means of easy sustenance. How dreadful the awful solitude must be, with life thus spent in patient endurance, year after year! The thought that I was returning to the land of plenty, with every comfort and enjoyment, made me feel all the more sensitive to the dreary joyless existence led by these distant tribes. Poor uncivilised human beings, left on the cold howling tundra! are they perhaps happier thus, living in ignorance of the pomps and vanities of our civilised world? Nature is all they can look to and live for. May they never know worse.

Time was now drawing on, and days were beginning to close in. We also were soon to take a last farewell of our Siberian surroundings, and direct our course once more homewards.

Final arrangements had been concluded. Captain Wiggins decided on accompanying the Russian fleet up the river to Yeneseisk, much to our regret, as his familiar voice and face would be sorely missed on our return voyage. The Russian naval officer, Lieutenant Dobrotvorscy, offered him a berth on board the paddle-steamer, where he was to meet with every kindness and attention.

On September 19th our stay, by no means without interest, was brought to a close. The three weeks anchored in the Yenesei River will ever remain a memorable feature of my youthful days, and in years to come will form an enduring and eventful episode in my life. My mind had certainly grown richer by a thousand new impressions, never likely to fade.

In the evening Captain Wiggins and the Russian officers came on board the *Blencathra* to bid us farewell. It was not without emotion that we parted after so many pleasant days. It seemed strange to imagine our little fleet thus split up, with only the *Orestes* and *Blencathra* to face the homeward voyage through the Kara Sea ; while, on the other hand, the three Russian vessels with three lighters in tow were to accomplish a voyage of 1500 miles up the river before ultimately reaching their destination. Up on deck late at night I witnessed for the last time the glorious evening closing in upon us, producing a strange effect on the surrounding scenery, which I am never likely to see again.

Before quitting this summer residence I feel compelled to say a few words of this grand and mighty river, the Yenesei. Siberia is drained by three large rivers, the Obi, Yenesei, and Lena, which form the most remarkable water-system in the world.

The Yenesei drains, of course, an enormous area, its remotest branches originating in Mongolia, in the Tannu Range of the Altai Mountains. According to geographical statistics, its length is given at about 3220 miles, and following a somewhat straight course, it discharges its waters into the Arctic Ocean. It is joined on its northerly course by several rivers, more especially on its right bank. The three principal towns situated on the Yenesei are Minusinsk, Krasnoiarsk, and Yeneseisk. At Golchika the river becomes narrower, extending barely over a breadth of four and a half miles. Shortly afterwards it expands like a lake, extending in width over more than forty miles, and forming a huge delta and lagoon, interspersed with low islands. The water, somewhat dark in colour, constitutes a pure fresh drink. The fishing, which is abundant, consists of white salmon, sturgeon, sterlet, herring, and several other kinds of fish, only known by their Russian names, such as muxoon, etc. The Yenesei is one of, if not the most, magnificent of rivers, in fact the immense volume of water which it pours forth probably exceeds that of any other river.

CHAPTER VII

ON September the 20th at 5 A.M. the *Orestes* and *Blencathra* weighed anchor from Golchika, to resume the homeward voyage.

Notwithstanding the early dawn, I cast a last glance of farewell on the little Russian fleet, which was also in readiness to get under way. It was a dull dreary day, snowing at intervals, and intensely cold. The scenery looked more dismal than ever. The *Blencathra* sailed and steamed alternately until the evening, when the *Orestes* took us in tow.

The *Orestes*, in the absence of the well-known figure on her bridge, was now under command of Captain Furneaux, a keen and able seafaring man, who, although these polar regions were unfamiliar to him, acquitted himself most admirably.

At 6.30 P.M. we were off Port Dickson ; the night was frigid indeed, and I began to realise the feeling suggestive of an arctic winter.

My diary on the 21st September gives our position in latitude 73°.43′, sighting a good deal of ice, slackening speed and steering carefully. Towards evening a strong westerly wind sprung up, with frequent thick showers of snow. Barometer 29.40. The following day, 22nd September, the wind had freshened into a strong breeze, occasioning a very uneasy motion. The cold had become severe. The thermometer marked 20 degrees of frost, undoubtedly the coldest day experienced during the whole of the voyage. The bows of the *Orestes* and *Blencathra* were covered with a thick coating of ice, from the tow-rope hung huge icicles, fringing also the deck and rigging, and producing quite a fairy-like appearance.

Had it not been for the pitching and rolling,

I should greatly have enjoyed this fantastic sight. My diary on September 23rd records a heavy gale of wind, strong head-sea, with fog and rain.

We were unable to do anything except listen to the wind as it howled through the rigging, seeming only to become more penetrating at every fresh burst. The waves dashing against the ship, however, seemed to distract me, as I lay tossing miserably about in my berth, unable to find a centre of gravity to escape the continual undulating roll, but without any uneasiness resulting from a sense of insecurity.

No doubt the steady old *Pandora*, with her trustworthy crew, had filled me with implicit confidence, which was fully maintained to the very end.

At first, I will admit, unaccustomed to yachting, and quite a novice at sea, the slightest motion or noise used immediately to arouse my apprehensions, and I nervously asked, to the amusement of the sailors, " Is it safe?" A little experience, however, soon taught me there was no danger likely to occur which I could not meet with coolness and self-possession. Such is the lesson of experience at sea.

At 9 P.M. the tow-rope snapped, under the weight, no doubt, of the heavy-laden icicles. Accordingly we steamed apart and lost sight of one another, the *Orestes* seeming bent on a different course.

On September 24th the gale at last subsided into a calm. I rose early and went up on deck, but soon had to repair below again. Ice was being shaken down in great quantities from the rigging. The temperature was still very low, and a nasty fog was beginning to close in upon us.

In the course of the afternoon we sighted a considerable amount of ice, and steamed through large ice-floes, meandering, so to speak, in the midst of them. The effect was strikingly weird. Being of a soft kind, however, the drift ice presented no difficulty, the *Blencathra* being a yacht specially adapted for such navigation.

We even went so far as to put her utmost capabilities to the test, for meeting with a large

sheet of ice ahead, we steered boldly at and successfully through it. The shock, however, was
apparent. Towards noon the fog, which had
hung densely around, gradually lifted, disclosing
a lovely gloriously-coloured sunset.

It was whispered that our position at that
moment was uncertain. We had kept steering a
south-west course, but still with no charts to refer
to, and an unreliable compass, we were more or
less in ignorance as to our whereabouts.

Owing also to the fog no observations could
be taken, and land not being visible, all seemed
desolation, wild and dreary.

Accordingly we dropped anchor at 10 P.M.,
hoping with dawn to resume our course. The
following morning, 25th September, anchor was
weighed at 5.30 A.M. The fog was again thick.
We were steaming slowly, and kept the lead
going continually in from five to seven fathoms
of water.

During the course of the forenoon, however,
as I was sitting down below writing my diary,
a curious grating sound and sudden stopping of

F. LEVBOURNE POPHAM.

To face page 92.

the engines suggested our having gone aground, and to rush up on deck was of course only a matter of a few seconds.

Shortly afterwards, with the fog gradually lifting, we found ourselves barely a few yards from the shore, which turned out to be the familiar bleak coast-line of Waigatz Island.

No time was lost in lowering a boat to ascertain the condition of the tide.

Great excitement prevailed, which helped to break the long monotony of the voyage through the Kara Sea.

With characteristic instinctiveness and quickness of perception Mr. Popham carried out his ideas, and steering the *Blencathra* full speed ahead, and then full speed astern, realised his anticipations.

We were once more afloat, and, owing to the sandy soil, the *Blencathra* escaped unscathed.

Meanwhile the natives of Waigatz Island had turned out on the beach—a motley crowd of men, women, and children—to witness our doings.

Their curiosity resulted in four Samoyedes rowing towards us, and shortly afterwards one

after the other clambered on board. Needless
to add that their delight was great, and their
surprise still greater, as they calmly watched the
crew's proceedings.

Finally the fog lifted entirely, and once more we
were directing our course towards Khabarova,
the little village which had witnessed, on our outward journey, our first acquaintance with Siberian
territory and its natives. As we dropped anchor
off this quaint fishing station we were greeted by
a familiar figure sitting in a Berthon boat.

Much to our surprise we recognised Mr.
Jackson.

We had, it will be remembered, deposited him
among the Samoyedes, his intention being to
explore the unknown inland peninsula of Yalmal,
and to spend a winter there, in the hope of
ultimately putting into execution his projects with
regard to the North Pole.

He came on board and enlivened us all with
an account of his varied experiences since
bidding us farewell.

He had only just returned from exploring the

Waigatz Island, accompanied by a Samoyede and his wife as guides. The fact of his having so far abandoned his previously settled intention with respect to Yalmal, was owing to the ground not being as yet covered with its thick white mantle, thus rendering locomotion by means of sledge and reindeer somewhat precarious.

He seemed quite happy amongst the Samoyedes, although he had neither friend nor companion, and was in entire ignorance of their language.

A Russian sloop happened to be lying at anchor at Khabarova, which accounted for the Samoyedes being all more or less in a bacchanalian condition, a plentiful supply of spirit having been obtained from the Muscovite ship.

Mr. Jackson, whose acquaintance with their habits was the result of personal association and experience, gave us miserable accounts of their devotion to spirits, such as vodka, and a decoction dignified by the name of brandy. So strong is this craving that they are ready to barter everything they possess in order to gratify their passion for drink.   Such demoralisation forms a sad comment on the practice of carrying civilisation to otherwise unsophisticated and simple-minded tribes.

Meanwhile the *Orestes* had not yet turned up, since parting company with us in the Kara Sea.

Mr. Jackson dined and slept on board, which he seemed thoroughly to enjoy after such a long spell of roughing it.

On the following day, 26th September, the *Orestes* appeared on the horizon, and in a couple of hours was lying at anchor beside us.

We had not quitted the yacht to go ashore, but the steward had gone to bargain for reindeer tongues, which were to form our staple food for the next few days.   Indeed, they were delicious, exquisitely flavoured, and a great delicacy, which I not only appreciated from a "gourmet" point of view, but from the novelty, to me, attached to them.   I cared less for the venison itself.

Time was now pressing, and late autumnal

weather setting in, which greatly diminishes the charm of yachting.

We were anxious to get on, and accordingly, once again in tow of the *Orestes*, we took leave of Mr. Jackson, the Samoyedes, and Siberia, and steamed through the Pet or Yugor Straits, bound for Archangel. The reason of this deviation in our homeward voyage was owing to the *Orestes* having been unable to discharge all the rails on the lighters at Golchika, and she was therefore carrying a cargo of 1100, to be trans-shipped at Archangel.

Far from being disappointed at this change in our programme, I was greatly pleased at the thought of seeing a Russian seaport, which had been pictured to me as not only of commercial importance but of interesting surroundings.

On the 27th of September the usual motion at sea again upset me, and although far from pleasant, I began to look upon sea-sickness merely as a matter of course, to be borne with complete indifference, and have certainly come to the

H

conclusion that no remedy has been found to cure this weakness.

We were now steaming through the waters of the Barents Sea, which was particularly devoid of any interest or excitement. A dense fog hung heavily around, and it was cold, raw, and damp.

The days were particularly uneventful,—no sound to be heard but the surging of the waves and the thump of the engines.

On the 28th of September it turned brighter, but yet no land was to be seen, and no vessels being met with in our course rendered our loneliness still more complete.

As I paced the decks the various aspects of the sea brought home to me a familiar passage, which I here take occasion to quote :—

> Turn to the watery world, but who to thee
> (A wonder yet unviewed) shall paint the sea—
> Various and vast, sublime in all its forms,
> When lulled by zephyrs, or when roused by storms ;
> Its colours changing, when from clouds and sun
> Shades after shades upon the surface run,
> Embrowned and horrid now, and then serene
> In limpid blue, and evanescent green,
> And oft the foggy banks on ocean lie,
> Lift the fair sail, and cheat the experienced eye.

In anticipation of a return to more civilised society we spent much of our time on deck, talking to the skipper and sailors, with their endless stock of adventures, anecdotes, and yarns, or else down below in the main cabin, reading arctic adventures or playing familiar airs, never before heard in these remote regions.

After rounding Cape Kanin we found ourselves coasting along the Kola Peninsula, and, entering on September 29th the White Sea or Bieloie More, we were once more within reach of our destination. Russian fishing-crafts now kept sailing by in large numbers, awakening in us quite a spirit of delight at the approach of a grand seaport. English steamers were also to be seen laden with timber from Archangel homeward bound. At 4 P.M. we were off Cape Orlov, presenting by its conspicuous lighthouse a feature on the otherwise unbroken sombre coast-line of the Kola Peninsula.

The White Sea was very calm as we steamed along on its pellucid waters, but I am told it is often subject to frightful squalls and storms, which lash the coast with great fury. The width of the inland sea in some parts is considerable, and, while coasting along, the opposite shore is invisible : navigation is only open during four months of the year.

About the 20th of October winter sets in, making a sudden irruption without prelude or warning. The White Sea is entirely frozen over in a very short time, and remains so until the breaking up of the ice at the end of May.

On the 30th September we were steaming along the eastern shore, and were delighted to be once more within limit of luxurious vegetation, after gazing for so many weeks on barren scenery.

Indeed, as we moved south, the shore gradually opened to us the aspect of thick forests of pine and fir trees. Meanwhile the crew were busy polishing up the decks, dabbing paint here and there, and trimming up the ship so spick and span, to look as if we were on an easy summer cruise, rather than returning from a perilous expedition to the remote waters of the Great Yenesei.

At noon we stopped alongside Morjovet Island, where was stationed a light-ship, with a signal flying, denoting pilots to be had. Shortly afterwards we saw a boat rowing towards us with Russian Custom-House officers. Their first question on approaching us was with regard to our health; secondly, whence we hailed. The answer, " From the Yenesei River, Siberia," pronounced with pride and emphasis, completely took them aback. They gazed at us in amazement, and not till after we had repeated the same reply over and over again did they seem to understand.

We then began to realise that we had actually achieved something to be proud of, by a voyage which we had hitherto regarded as nothing remarkable, owing to the comfortable and delightful auspices under which it had been conducted.

Taking a pilot on board for navigation up the river Dwina, we resumed our course.

The *Orestes* had dropped the tow-rope and was heading us.

Crossing the bar, we entered the mouth of the

river, and gradually became enraptured by its winding course, at times so narrow that the banks looked as if likely to close. in upon us at every turn. The steering was excellent, and we all clustered near the helm in admiration of the brave old pilot's skill, by which we threaded and glided through the sinuosities and intricate navigation of our passage. The scenery was magnificent, the trees exhibiting varied hues of brilliant autumnal colouring. I cannot remember to have ever been so much impressed by the beauties of nature. Perhaps the dreary Siberian soil having been for so many weeks the object of my daily gaze somewhat accounted for this burst of enthusiasm.

The weather had turned exceedingly mild, and the evening was glorious.

At 6 P.M. we finally reached Solombola, and dropped anchor off this island, situated at only a short distance from Archangel and connected with it by means of a bridge. Business being, as a rule, conducted here, accounted for our not lying off Archangel.

No sooner had we dropped anchor than we thought of going ashore. The Custom-House officers, however, not having been on board to conclude the necessary formalities, no one was allowed to quit the ship.

Eventually they turned up. Two of them appeared in uniform, accompanied by an interpreter. We were thoroughly cross-questioned, and our respective answers put down on paper.

The ladies' presence particularly puzzled them. They could not believe we had thus voluntarily accompanied the expedition to the Yenesei, braved the perils of the Kara Sea, and all dangers attached to arctic exploration. I suppose they looked upon us as very eccentric beings; but I afterwards heard that we were the subjects of much admiration and astonishment, on account of the dangers and the novelty of our enterprise.

CHAPTER VIII

THE city of Archangel, situated on the right bank of the river North Dwina, was founded in 1584 under the name of New Cholmagor; twenty-nine years later the name was changed to that of Archangel, from the monastery dedicated to the Archangel Michael. The province is three times the size of England, and stretches from the Lapland coast to the Ural Mountains, including the islands of Kolguiev, Waigatz, and Novaia Zemlia. The population of 338,715 inhabitants includes Korelians, Zirians, Samoyedes, and Lapps. Archangel's chief historical importance lies in the fact of its having been the first and for a long

time the only port of Russia. The distinguished
and ill-fated explorer, Chancellor, touched there
with his expedition, from which time dates the
importance of the place from a commercial point
of view.

In 1693 Peter the Great visited Archangel,
and built there the first Russian ship, besides an
Admiralty House and a wharf at Solombola. At
the beginning of this century, in the reign of
Alexander I., Archangel was most thriving and
of great importance, owing to Napoleon having
closed all the ports of Europe against English
ships with the exception of Archangel, so that a
large trade was actively carried on with Great
Britain. From the time of the Crimean war,
however, when an English squadron under the
command of Captain Erasmus Ommany block-
aded the White Sea and stopped all commerce,
the trade of Archangel declined. The English
colony left, Germans took their place, and so far
it has never recovered the blow. " But times are
altered, trades unfeeling train " has passed to
younger and more active rivals, and while newer

and less inaccessible ports have enjoyed the advantages of a later civilisation, the ancient seat of Russia's foreign trade is still almost an outcast from all. More than 600 miles sever Archangel from all railway communication, and only one telegraphic wire at present connects it with the capital. Such trade as exists is now mostly carried on by English steamers, of which 90 to 130 visit the port each season, whilst, on account of the heavy tax recently imposed on German ships, an increase of tariff dues amounting from ten kopeks per ton to two roubles, the German commercial trade is almost completely extinguished. The chief article of export is timber, imports being very limited, as nearly all ships come in with ballast after discharging coal at Norwegian ports on their way.

In old days officials in disgrace were banished to Archangel, while in the present day those who are found guilty of dishonest practices are sent here, with perfect liberty to go where they like or to do what they like, provided they remain in the district. Almost all the business people of Archangel are of German extraction, very few of English origin, but at present their families are mostly Russianised in feeling and habits.

The morning following our arrival at Solombola, the 1st of October, we resolved to drive over to Archangel to gain an impression of Russian life, as it is presented in this ancient seaport. Several droshkis had been ordered, and the weather having turned exceedingly mild, we were full of joyous expectations.

The droshkis are most curious-looking vehicles, unfitted with a hood, and generally so small that two people can barely occupy with ease and comfort the space allotted to each. On the other hand, some are constructed much after the fashion of an Irish jaunting car, on which travellers sit back to back, journeying along sideways, when no little adroitness is required to keep yourselves steady on your seats; but those who have acquired the art of cleverly adjusting themselves to the situation, hold that it is a very comfortable vehicle, and by no means unsociable, in spite of appearances to the contrary.

Off we went in our respective droshkis, bump-
ing and jolting most fearfully over uneven roads,
falling and rising occasionally in and out of a deep
rut with a crash and a bump that sent the mud
splashing all over us. The little Russian ponies
are very speedy, and tore off at quite an alarming
rate, landing us in a very short time in Archangel.
Our impression was in many respects not in accordance with our anticipations.

The town, as we approached it, presented on
the whole and at first sight a most decayed and
squalid appearance. The streets are dirty, and
the pavements little better. However, a confused
mass of buildings, minarets, and churches, with
their star-spangled domes and gold crosses flash-
ing in the sun, offered rather a pretty *coup d'œil*.
Very few houses built of stone are to be seen ; they
are mostly of wood, consist but of one floor, and
present a most picturesque aspect with their
emerald green and crushed-strawberry coloured
wooden roofs. This harmonious blending of
delicate tints gives an agreeable colouring to the
natural features of the town, of which the principal

street is Troitski Prospect, and on further acquaintance we thought the panorama extremely pretty,
and quite unlike anything we had ever seen before.
What struck me on first passing through the
streets was, to all outward appearance, the entire
absence of shops, which as a rule give so much
local colouring and life to a place. Of course
there are shops, but from the outside they are un-
recognisable, as no goods are displayed in the windows. I was told that this is a custom throughout
most Russian towns, where the intense cold during the winter months necessitates double and
sometimes treble windows.

For lunch we directed our steps to what we
were told to be the best restaurant in Archangel,
the approach to which was far from tempting.
However we went in. A large collection of
tradespeople and peasants were sitting at separate
tables, enjoying a curious sort of repast of pickled
cucumbers and vodka. The heat was overpowering, and we had again to undergo a former
experience of a musty stuffy atmosphere with a
curious smell prevailing of something like rotten

leather.   Notwithstanding these drawbacks, we sat down to our lunch.   The beer, called quass, manufactured from fermented grain and greatly relished by the Russians, was pronounced to be very good.

During our repast a band performed.   Russian music is intensely melancholy, most of the national melodies being in the minor key, wailing and lamenting, with little time or rhythm, like those of the Tsiganes.

After our experience of the oppressive atmosphere and strange surroundings we departed to seek for curiosities, in search of shops where such may be found, but in that respect Archangel is very deficient.   We first directed our steps towards the Museum, a tumble-down miserable-looking building, containing three or four small rooms crowded with all sorts of relics.   The strangest object that interested me most was the skeleton of a mammoth.   I only wished the flesh-less monster could have answered a few questions as to the life of his time, and how he got on with primitive man, whether he had to work for his living under human domination, or how many men he had killed, and who or what killed him. These and a few more questions it would be interesting to have answered by an intelligent mammoth with a good memory.

At 5 P.M. we attended the Greek service at the Cathedral, which forms a conspicuous feature in the square. The outer walls are decorated with paintings of religious subjects, and the spires are of gilt with emerald-green tints freely displayed. The interior presented a most gaudy appearance, with much richness of decoration and massive gold ikons plastered with gems. The priest was robed in gorgeous vestments, and conducted the service in a very solemn manner, earnest and impressive. There being no seats, the congregation necessarily stood during the service, only varying their position by a constant dropping on the knees, prostrating their foreheads to the ground, and making the sign of the cross, the reverse way to the Roman Catholic devotee. As in all Greek Churches, the Cathedral service was devoid of instrumental music ; only vocal sounds

are to be heard, which, indeed, are most melo-
dious.   The choir contained two splendid bass
voices, the effect of which was very grand.

At the conclusion of the service, about 6.30 P.M.,
we walked towards Solombola, but, with no
artificial light in the streets, we could hardly
grope our way about on the wooden pavement,
not in quite as smooth a condition as might have
been wished.   So we called a droshki, a shabby
vehicle, one of those shaped like the Irish car ;
and so, back to back, we homeward sped.

Far from finding it cold at Archangel, we
enjoyed during the whole of our stay a spell of
very mild weather, so that we were enabled to
steam about in our little launch every day, towards
the town, where a fair happened to be going on,
in which a motley crowd was to be seen, giving
one a very good idea of national life.   A varied
assortment of articles for household use and
personal adornment was displayed, also furs and
leather goods, the unpleasant odour from which I
have already alluded to.   As I had acquired the
knowledge of a few Russian words, I now made

ARCHANGEL FROM THE DWINA.

To face page 112

some purchases, amongst other things, as a
curiosity, of several wooden spoons used by the
Russian peasants to eat their food, and while at
Golchika I had the honour of being presented
with one by the priest of Turukhansk. What
particularly took my fancy was a peculiar fur,
which I was told was very rare, called *vulpes*
crucigera, a variety of the *canis vulpes;* of a soft
gray colour with a beautifully marked black cross
down the back. It is the fur of quite young foxes,
who, when they grow older, completely change
their colour. As a rule it is a mistake to suppose
that good furs can be purchased only in Russia,
for most of these are sent to England, and it is a
fact that even Russians come to London for their
furs, where they are much better made up than in
their own country.

One afternoon as we were walking along the
quay we happened to see a yacht at anchor near
Archangel. On approaching, it turned out to be
the *Nordenskiold*, belonging to Mr. Siberiakoff.
With our usual inquisitiveness we proposed going
on board and having a look round, when the

I

Russian captain appearing on deck, invited us to his cabin and received us with warm hospitality. Champagne was instantly ordered, and we did not fail to drink to the health and to the well-being of a country and people from whom we had met with such kindness and cordiality. Afterwards we sat some time conversing with the captain, who had a very good knowledge of German, which greatly facilitated our intercourse, until, as it began to get dusk, we bade adieu to our friendly host. Judging from our experience, there can be no people in the world who are more genuinely kind and hospitable to strangers than the Russians. They possess in an eminent degree that ease and grace of manner, and an undefinable attraction which is so socially captivating.

Leaving the *Nordenskiold*, we walked towards the landing stage, to find our little steam-launch ready to convey us back to Solombola. Never shall I forget the exquisite beauty of that homeward trip, under an indigo sky irradiated with millions of shimmering worlds, each one seeming to be a gigantic diamond, the brilliancy of which darkened the neighbouring spaces to illimitable and mystic depths. We then glided swiftly through the still placid waters studded with the reflection of countless glittering stars. The spires and buildings of the city clustering round the golden dome of the Cathedral loomed out in the twilight with enhanced size and grandeur, yet at the same time clear and distinct as at noonday, more like a dream than a waking experience, whilst the mildness of the atmosphere gave an additional charm.

Archangel, viewed from the river, at some distance, forms a lovely picture which, alas, fades almost immediately on stepping into its midst, for the love of vodka seems to reign supreme among the people, and too frequently one is shocked by the sight of victims to excessive indulgence in this prevalent taste.

The surroundings of Archangel are exceedingly pretty. Numbers of picturesque little islands are to be seen dotted promiscuously about on the north bank of the Dwina, and of an afternoon we often employed our time in exploring them. There is excellent shooting to be had on the mainland : of wild animals may be mentioned the bear, wolf, fox, reindeer, hare, etc. But few people visit Archangel, and only two English yachts have been there during the last six or seven years, the *Thistle*, belonging to the Duke of Hamilton, and the *Blencathra*.

Before leaving Archangel, Mr. James was asked to join a shooting expedition. These excursions generally take place on a Sunday. The party consisted of half a dozen sportsmen. They called for Mr. James at 8 P.M., and steamed up the Dwina in a little steam-launch. The whole night was spent in playing cards, drinking, and smoking till 4 A.M. on Sunday morning, when the destination having been reached they all landed to begin their day's shooting. Beaters had been provided beforehand, consisting of a number of little boys, who with cowbells made enough noise to frighten any one out of their senses. This commotion, however, conduced to the desired result. Notwithstanding the effects of dissipated hours, the sport was conducted with great success, lasting from early dawn till twilight, the party returning late on Sunday.

The British Vice-Consul, Mr. Cooke, who has been here for many years, was full of amiable attentions, and contributed much to the thorough enjoyment we derived from our stay. He recommended a visit to the Monastery of Solavetski, the Mecca of Russia, situated on an island in the White Sea, at some short distance from Kem on the coast of Lapland. Owing to our sudden departure from Archangel we were obliged, much to our regret, to give up the idea of paying the Monastery a visit. This Monastery, it may be remembered, the British squadron attempted to bombard in 1854, but the shrieks of the sea-gulls, like the geese of the Capitol, warded off the disaster, and they have been looked upon ever since as sacred birds.

Meantime the *Orestes* was being laden with a freight of timber. Having seen to all final arrangements, we thought of resuming our homeward course, and leaving her to follow under the

command of Captain Furneaux. It was, however, with a feeling of regret that we parted
company after we had acted as convoy to her
ever since leaving Vardoe.

Notwithstanding the unfavourable and unpleasant impression produced on first acquaintance with Archangel, I must admit that with
time the place began to grow upon one,
and on leaving I carried away with me a
hope that this, my first introduction to Russia,
might not be the last, and that Archangel would
be the stepping - stone to future visits. The
germs of love of travel and adventure seem
so readily to take root that I have every reason
to cherish the thought of the realisation of my
wishes.

CHAPTER IX

HOMEWARD BOUND!

It was with a feeling of irrepressible delight that I welcomed the familiar sound of the weighing of the anchor at Solombola at 8.30 A.M. on the 12th October. It was getting unpleasantly cold and damp, days were closing in, very much curtailing our favourite saunters on deck, which after all constitutes much of the enjoyment of a sea-cruise. Our stock of chatter had by this time been considerably drawn upon, our music had been played and strummed over and over again, books of travel and science had been read, digested, and discussed more than once, in fact

we had rather fallen short of resources for
mutual amusement or instruction. However, the
thought of returning once more safe and sound
to one's home associations, to be the object of
" much ado " by friends and relations, in other
words, to have accomplished something out of
the common, produced in me a feeling of satisfaction and contentment which, after all, is pleas-
ing to every one, notwithstanding the strong
flavour of vanity which it is sure to imply. But
youth has the advantages of youth, and among
them indulgence from those of riper years.

Onward we steamed down the river Dwina,
piloted by the same old Muscovite we had had
previously. The fog being thick, we had to
bring up at 11.30 A.M., and not till 3 P.M. were
we able to proceed. During the course of the
afternoon we dropped our pilot at the light-
ship. Once again we were in the White Sea,
enjoying a delightful calm, which contrasted
all the more cruelly with the fearful gale we were
about to experience on entering the Murmanian
Sea, all the way to Vardoe. The object of our

returning to this "fishy" little island was to pick up letters ; we had been without news since last quitting Norway, and we were pining to hear what had taken place in England and abroad since entrusting our precious lives to the unknown mysteries of polar regions.

After passing Cape Orlov a fair wind set in, and gradually freshened into a strong north-east breeze, with snow squalls. The rolling of the ship from side to side was positively alarming, beating the record since our first setting out to sea. I could not quit my bed for fear of being pitched all over the place, but my work was amply cut out and my strength fully put to the test in trying to hold on to my mattress, an exercise lasting fully twenty-four hours, with the impossibility of snatching a few minutes' rest. How I did pity the poor man at the wheel, steering bravely through the snowstorms and squalls ! My fate, after all, was nothing compared to his situation. However, all things pleasant and unpleasant come to an end, and great was my relief when we steamed into the familiar harbour of Vardoe, dropping anchor in its quiet waters at 11.30 A.M. on the 15th of October.

All my miseries were soon forgotten on being the recipient of a bundle of letters from friends and relations. How I relished the contents! If they had caused any waste of time to the senders, they would indeed have felt fully recompensed could they have witnessed the appreciation and welcome showered upon their act of kindness. The harbour - master came on board to conduct the usual formalities, and Mr. Holmboe, the British Consul, called to welcome us back again from the icy regions, seeming amazed to see us so well and bright after all the perilous experiences he associated with our expedition.

Vardoe, this time, appeared to us under quite a different aspect, the harbour being deserted by its hundreds of fishing craft, which had presented during the season a very picturesque feature. The little island was sprinkled over with a white coating of snow, and the air, impregnated as usual with the odours I have described, was on

this occasion particularly devoid of unpleasant-
ness. Our stay this time was but of short
duration. We weighed anchor that same afternoon, and committed ourselves to the extreme
north of Europe.

Changes of weather are sudden in these latitudes.
By three o'clock the wind had dropped as if by
magic, and once again we enjoyed smooth waters.
The deck was covered with ice and snow, looking
arctic indeed. After dinner I enjoyed a stroll
on deck. The heavens presented a sight far too
grand and imposing to describe. The night was
remarkably illumined by myriads of stars, perhaps
worlds, as astronomers might say, but the Polar
Star outshone its feebler neighbours with such
brilliancy as by comparison to materially eclipse
their splendour.

The greatest phenomenon in the Arctic
Circle is undoubtedly the effect produced by the
aurora borealis, whose magic splendour naturally
excited the keenest observation. No one has
been able to paint in words this extraordinary
vision, which seems to strike a chord in the heart

of the spectator. They whose roaming imagination has not yet led them to feast on its glories, more especially enjoyed by arctic explorers, should not hesitate to seek the North Cape, where its grandeur is displayed in unwonted magnificence.

The following morning I was up on deck at early dawn to enjoy the pure exhilarating air, and the majestic outline of the rocky peninsula of Nord Kyn, the most northerly point of continental Europe. The weather was lovely, throwing into bold relief the sombre cliffs, around which hundreds of screeching sea-birds awakened in the solemn stillness weird mysterious echoes. The atmosphere was like that of the finest crystal, not a cloud to fleck the sky. The scenery was indeed romantic and grand, and as we steamed onward this glorious panorama never left us.

It will be remembered that on our outward voyage we missed seeing the North Cape, our course having taken us through a narrow fjord separating the mainland from the star-shaped island of Mageroe. Very soon we found ourselves rounding the Cape, which presented itself

THE NORTH CAPE.

From a Sketch by F. Leybourne Popham.

To face page 124.

to us in the shape of a headland, a huge mass
of dark mica slate rising a thousand feet perpen-
dicularly from the cold Arctic Sea, backed in the
distance by snowy mountain heights sparkling in
the rays of sunshine as if cut out in silver against
the solid blue of the sky. The accompanying
illustration, from a sketch by Mr. Popham, gives
a very good idea of the shape and form. I do not
think this imposing scene can ever be obliterated
from my memory, for I was overwhelmed with the
majesty of such a glorious sight, witnessed under
such truly favourable circumstances. Spell-bound,
I sat on deck in presence of the sublime and wonderful works of nature, in silent thought. I felt
as though my eyes were peering into the unseen, as
though I were on the threshold of a new world,
teeming with unknown perils. All my sympathies
were with those gallant explorers who have risked
their lives for the advancement of science and
challenged an untoward fate in the hope of obtaining an advantage for mankind. Yes, indeed, we
cannot sufficiently admire such heroic enterprises.
And now that I can in a modest way number

myself among arctic voyagers, I am able in some slight degree to picture to myself the numerous and perilous obstacles to be overcome. May the Norwegian Dr. Nansen, in his endeavour to solve the greatest problem in the world, meet with every success, assured of the warmest sympathy of the civilised world for the realisation of his venturesome enterprise.

In the course of the afternoon we sighted a small fishing craft with two fishermen busily engaged in hauling up the nets, and eager to enjoy some fresh fish we steamed towards them, and lowering the canvas boat, the steward rowed off to obtain what he could, returning after a few minutes with a variety of cod, haddock, and halibut, weighing in all 121 lbs., for which he paid the modest sum of two kroner (2s.)

Shortly afterwards we saw the conspicuous lighthouse of Fruholm, situated on the island of Ingo, the most northerly lighthouse in the world, and a welcome beacon to the adventurous voyager, as he is wafted to his still more northerly destination. With even still greater welcome does he regard, almost as a personal friend, the cheerful guiding light as he returns on his homeward way. Towards evening the setting sun produced a fairy-like appearance, tinging the white summits of the glorious glaciers and their extensive snowfields with a pale rosy hue. Instead of steering our course in a westerly tack, it was settled that our homeward route was to be due south, between the mainland and the islands, which form as it were a gigantic breakwater along the entire western coast of Norway. This decision raised my spirits, for I had looked upon the North Sea at this late autumnal season as associated with grim and dreadful gales, and to think that we were to experience delightful smooth waters all through the fjords was indeed most welcome, in addition to the expectation of enjoying lovely scenery.

At 6.30 P.M. we sighted a brilliant electric illumination to our left, which proved to be Hammerfest. Just as we were steering towards the town to drop anchor for the night a pleasant alternative suggested itself. Being a clear moon-light night, the pilot proposed taking us straight on to Tromsoe; and accordingly we steamed on afresh and directed our course through the Sörö Sund, and, viewed only by the light of the heavens, the scene was fantastically weird. The navigation is at all times intricate and dangerous, but especially so during the winter nights, which had begun to close in at quite an early hour. Not to lose a single grand sight of the ever-changing panorama we were all up on deck at early dawn. Where indeed does nature present more variety of picturesque aspect than in the fjords of Norway, or its beauties appeal so intensely to one's sympathies?

It was bitterly cold, with many degrees of frost. The morning was, however, bright and sunny, and the scenery quite magnificent. Finally, we anchored off Tromsoe at 1.30 P.M. Our object was to drop several ice-masters, as we found we had no occasion to avail ourselves of their services. After lunch we went ashore to renew acquaintance with the little town. It looked very much deserted. Most of the inhabitants had taken to their cosy houses, and were to be seen (through the windows) collected in family groups round the large stove, which in these northern latitudes forms the main feature of a Norwegian household. The Lapps, too, who had been of conspicuous interest on our previous visit, had left the town to return to their settlements on the mountains and roam about in their characteristic fashion. They exhibit a wonderful display of vigour and vitality, which somewhat accounts for the way in which they can brave the rigour of the long winter months without injury to their health, although it gives them a prematurely aged look. We strolled about, and were particularly struck with the bright and cleanly appearance of the town. In the afternoon we went into the Grand Hotel to take a cup of coffee, having been warned against the Norwegian notion of making tea. Bread and cheese we found very good, but curiously enough we could obtain no fresh butter, which is not manufactured in such remote latitudes, but has to be imported salted from the south. Towards evening we returned on board, a

K

pink glow tinging all the surrounding snowy peaks.

The following day, 18th of October, we were still to remain at anchor, some business having to be transacted with the Consul. We therefore took occasion to visit the Museum, which we had heard was full of interesting specimens of all kinds. So extensive had it become of late years, that a building on a much larger scale than the present edifice was being erected at some short distance off. We were highly interested, particularly in all the arctic curiosities, of which we were beginning to feel ourselves connoisseurs.

Instead of returning on board for luncheon, we determined upon trying the Norwegian fashion of *table d'hôte* at two o'clock, since we never before had experienced their cooking. The courses opened with fish, and next came beef with *compôte*, such as is commonly associated with German diet, an incongruous mixture, to which I never could get quite reconciled. The beer was very good, with a delicate flavour of pine. Before returning on board we

enjoyed a lively walk through a birch-tree forest
up on the hills.

A pilot had meanwhile been engaged to take
us down to Bergen, and next morning anchor
was weighed at 6 A.M. It was very foggy, and
a heavy snowstorm obliged us to remain down
below and occupy our thoughts as best we could.
I set to work to obtain by dint of perseverance
a slight knowledge of the Norwegian language,
of which I soon acquired a smattering, many
words having a strong resemblance to German,
but sounding if possible more guttural, and like
a bad *patois*. It was damp and cheerless indeed!
However, I was thankful to enjoy smooth water,
and not to be tossing about on the ocean, as
a strong gale of wind howling with great fury
outside suggested to us might have been the
case. Owing to the night being very dark, we
were obliged to bring up at the small station of
Kastnaeshaven, and proceed the following morning at 6 A.M. We steamed through the Vaags
and Jiel Fjord, the scenery upon the mainland presenting mountains piled up in irregular groups,

and cliffs rising from the water on either side sheer and abrupt; yet whenever a green patch was to be seen a few huts were sure to be found clustering together at the foot of some stupendous mass of rock, giving colour to the view, which would otherwise have looked un-utterably desolate.

Not being able to fetch another anchorage before dark, the pilot, a cautious old sailor, suggested spending the night at Lödingen, prettily situated on " Hindo " Island.   Accord-ingly anchor was dropped at 3.30 P.M.   We went ashore to have a brisk walk so as to keep ourselves warm.   The chief building, situ-ated in the midst of half a dozen wooden houses, was a huge telegraph office, forming a very important station, in which many people are daily employed.   Whenever we landed numer-ous inquiries were made with regard to Dr. Nansen, and the general opinion seemed to be that if thorough knowledge, mature reflection, and indomitable pluck can secure success, he is most decidedly the man to achieve it.

The following day we proceeded through the
Vest Fjord. Owing to the mist, which hid the
famous view, we could only distinguish a faint
outline of the Lofoden Islands. Those numerous sharp peaks, covered with snow and set off
by a cloudless blue sky and dazzling sunshine,
would have been perfectly divine to behold.
The approach to Grötö, where the pilot brought
up early in the afternoon, was quite magnificent.
The majestic peak of the Skothammer rose high
and perpendicular to our left on the mainland,
and the navigation through a narrow inlet, interspersed with rocks, demanded quick and careful
steering. Grötö presented an exceedingly pretty
sheltered harbour, with most picturesque surroundings. In order to kill time, which was
beginning to hang heavily on our hands, on
account of the slow progress we were making,
we went for a walk on the beach. We also
took our dogs for a run, which they seemed
to enjoy quite as much as we did. Poor things
—five of them—they seemed to understand perfectly well each time we dropped anchor, and

sat on the edge of the ship, looking longingly towards the shore; so excited were they on nearing the beach that, one and all, they jumped into the icy cold water, and tore in wild spirits all over the place. On one occasion they chased and scared a whole herd of cows, which were driven for a considerable distance on the hills. The amazed inhabitants, half dormant perhaps at the approach of winter, soon appeared on the threshold of their wooden huts, not at first able to realise who had come at this remote season of the year to ruffle the calm simplicity of their lives. It was indeed a lively sight, and amused us immensely.

The following morning, on leaving Grötö, the navigation became most excitingly intricate. We had to steer through narrow channels, with rocks strewn about us in every direction. Unfortunately, the cold, damp weather greatly diminished the enjoyment of sitting for hours together upon deck to watch our course.

The panorama never ceased to be imposing. Although seen under unfavourable circumstances,

OUR ESKIMO DOG.

(From a Kodak Photograph.)

To face page 134.

the days being gloomy and the atmosphere
sometimes slightly misty, yet I think this sombre
colouring was in keeping with the savage grandeur
of the scenery. We had a splendid view of the
Sandhorn, which was covered with snow, as well
as of the Füglo Island. In the distance one
beholds a lovely chain of snowy mountains with
lofty peaks, or rather domes, towering high into
the heavens. No one has any idea of Norwegian
scenery unless they have been in the country.
Norway must be seen, it cannot be described.
The tourist season closes, as a rule, towards the
end of August; so steaming, as we did, at the end
of October, through the fjords, we came in for a
wintry aspect, in strong contrast to the bright
summer season of the ordinary tourist.

On October the 23rd we crossed the Arctic
Circle. It was, perhaps, not without a feeling of
satisfaction that we quitted the frigid zone to enter
a more temperate one. As we steamed along we
met with perpetual variety in form and feature;
so much so, that we never got tired of gazing at
nature's wonders. In the course of the after-

noon we dropped anchor at Sövig, quite a small hamlet.   It, however, deserves mention, being situated at the foot of one of the grandest mountains I have ever seen.   It is called Syv Söstre, or Seven Sisters, from the fact of its forming a chain with seven distinct successive peaks.

The following day we resumed our course. On leaving the charmingly situated village of Brönö, we passed through a crooked channel, scarcely wider than the yacht, to find ourselves in an almost land-locked bay.   Then we came in view of a famous mountain called Torghatten.   It has the appearance of a broad-brimmed hat, and as we approached we distinguished a curious tunnel through it.   The old pilot, a walking guide-book of the Norwegian fjords, informed us that at half its height it is perforated by an orifice, through which the light may distinctly be seen, the tunnel having a length of 540 feet.   As may be supposed, this curiously-shaped mountain is not without a legend.   The story goes, that two giants were rivals for a girl, and agreed to fight a duel with bows and arrows. One was pierced by an arrow, which, when it was drawn out, the dying giant threw about ten miles off, where it sank and became a rock. This rock is now avoided by ships, as very dangerous, and can only be seen at low tide. Torghatten is the dead giant, and the aperture is where the arrow was drawn from. Certainly the mountain forms one of the most conspicuous and striking features in the fjords.

For several successive days we steamed slowly on, anchoring over night off pretty little hamlets, and resuming our course at dawn. The cold rainy weather began to damp our spirits, till at last the approach of Trondhyem awakened in us new interests. Late at night, on October 30th, the yacht was moored inside the harbour, and the following day was spent in inspecting the town.

Trondhyem, now the second city of the kingdom, was the capital of Norway until the fourteenth century, and enjoyed considerable importance as a royal residence. It is said to have been founded in 996, under the name of Nidaros, after the river Nid, which appellation, however, was changed in the sixteenth century to that of Trondhyem. The patron saint is Olaf. The great glory of the town is concentrated in its old Cathedral.

From the Hotel Britannia we directed our steps towards the Munke Gade, which leads up to it. There we found a guide, who took us all round, and interested us immensely with all the information he imparted to us. Part of the building through which we had to pass is in ruins, but the work of restoration is now being actively carried on. The architecture is old Norman. Great richness of decoration is displayed, remarkable in detail, which is exquisite for execution, beauty, and purity of style. The arches are also most graceful. St. Olaf's Well is an interesting feature, so is the magnificent statue of Christ, by Thorwaldsen, placed in one of the niches. The Chapter-House forms a curious contrast to the transition period, being entirely devoid of richness of decoration of any kind. During the summer months it is generally given over to the English residents for divine service. The stone, quarried in the locality, is of a curious blue slate colour, of extreme hardness. The present king of Sweden, Oscar II., was crowned in this Cathedral in 1872. It is surrounded by a graveyard, which is now converted into a kind of pleasure-garden.

Besides lounging about the streets, which seemed particularly devoid of bustle and life, time and darkness prevented us from visiting any other sights. We returned to the Hotel Britannia for tea, and regained the yacht at 9.30 P.M. It was bitterly cold, with several degrees of frost. Our impression of Trondhyem was that of a sober dreary-looking town, and, apart from its Cathedral, showed little to impress us.

Early on 1st of November we were steaming once more through the Trondhyem Fjord, with a view to shaping our course straight for Dundee. However, as fate would have it, a head-wind set in, with a falling barometer. The pilot advised keeping to smooth waters inside the fjords, instead of beating against the wind in the North Sea. His advice was fully endorsed by me, for I dreaded the crossing in a rough sea. For several days more, the weather having cleared, we enjoyed the lovely wintry scenery of the fjords, which seemed to grow more magnificent with each successive hour.

Our next anchorage of importance was inside the sheltered harbour of Christiansund, an admirable landscape, grand and wild, with formidable peaks around, forming to my mind one of the most delightful spots in the fjords. Numerous picturesque fishing-smacks were to be seen lying at anchor. The town, of considerable dimensions, with 10,000 inhabitants or more, is curiously built in the shape of an amphitheatre. The surroundings are both graceful and enchanting, and we were told that a relation of a well-known English family has taken up his entire abode there, and never quits it, even during the long winter months.

Christiansund carries on an active trade in

fisheries, forming one of the most important stations in Norway. Its trade is chiefly with France and Spain.

The next day we were off the renowned and dreaded rock-strewn stretch of Hustadviken. Rocks are to be seen scattered about, barely showing above the water. We had a magnificent view of the Molde Fjord and its grand mountain scenery, forming one of the finest in Norway. Indeed it is difficult for me to give an adequate idea of what I feel utterly incapable to describe. The most graphic pen would fail to portray with justice the many fair and impressive scenes viewed from the yacht's deck.

Finally, however, on rounding the promontory of Statland, which juts out into the sea, the skipper sent word to say that a fair wind had set in, and taking advantage of it, he was making for Dundee instead of keeping to smooth water down to Bergen.

No sooner were we in the North Sea than my miseries began afresh. Squalls and hailstorms raged with violence, and we were rolled about

unmercifully. I was indeed wretched. Keeping
as best I could to my berth, I felt, although so
near, I might perhaps never see my home again,
and my anxiety at returning was greater than I
can describe. Hours dragged on ; the three days
seemed endless. For want of fresh air and something to do, I opened my port-hole to cool my
excitement, but before I had time to realise this
act of thoughtlessness, I found myself thoroughly
cooled down and well drenched as a punishment
for such imprudence. A huge wave had worked
its way into my cabin, volumes of water simply
inundating me and my berth. However, without losing presence of mind, I used all my
strength to close the port-hole. Shivering with
cold and helpless as a drowned rat, I called for
assistance to the steward, who arrived on the
scene much dismayed at my appearance. With his
usual attentiveness and quickness of action, all
was put right again in a very short time. I was
taken into a vacant cabin, much'amused at what
had happened, and completely cured of sea-
sickness! Thus, at the very close of our

long sea voyage, meeting with an efficacious remedy, though rather an awkward one to prescribe.

Gradually the bleak east coast-line of Scotland became visible. At 2 A.M. on the 7th of November we dropped anchor at Dundee, the termination of my first voyage at sea, a trip which had occupied nearly four months.

In conclusion, I cannot dwell sufficiently on the pleasure, knowledge, experience, and interest derived from this my first sea voyage and my first introduction to arctic regions. It has opened out a new sphere in my life, enlarged my mind, stimulated my enthusiasm for the beauties of nature,—in short, I have reaped from it benefits which will never die.

With keen appreciation have I committed to memory all the impressions, fresh and vivid, met with during these months of travel. Youth will fade, but these recollections of youthful days I shall, in years to come, always love to recall.

Chapters X. and XI. are contributed by Captain JOSEPH WIGGINS, and give an account of his journey after parting company with the BLEN- CATHRA at GOLCHIKA, and some remarks on the NANSEN EXPEDITION.

L

Photograph by E. Davey Lavender.   Bromley, Kent.
                        CAPTAIN JOSEPH WIGGINS.

To face page 147.

CHAPTER X

By the 20th of September we were in readiness to
proceed up river to Yeneseisk, the *Orestes* having
some thousand or more rails left in her, which
were to be taken to Archangel and deposited
there, as was requested by the Russian Government before she left England.

We had also the great disappointment of
having to leave on shore at Golchika some
three hundred tons of excellent graphite, which
it was impossible to obtain, as there was no
remaining barge to bring it alongside. This
graphite had been sent down the river by Mr.
Chiromnick of Yeneseisk, as well as a large

quantity of timber for shipment to England. It now remains at Golchika for next year's transit.

The *Minusinsk* steamer had . already been despatched on her voyage up river, under the command of my brother, laden with wares and with valuable gold-mining machinery, some five days in advance, and bearing telegrams, etc., to report the position of affairs to St. Petersburg and London.

It was now the turn of the *Offtzine*, with myself on board, to try her luck with three laden barges and the schooner *Scuratoff* in tow. At 8 A.M. on September the 21st she parted company with the *Blencathra* and *Orestes*, which returned to the Kara Sea, but fresh troubles soon overtook her. A heavy gale from the north-west, accompanied by thick blinding snowstorms, burst upon her just at the critical time, when she was in a most difficult passage surrounded by shallows.

The *Graff Ignatieff*, with the *Scuratoff* in tow, returned at once, and succeeded in gaining shelter near the previous anchorage. The *Offtzine* continued, with the *Malyguine* and *Bard*, and she succeeded in groping her way up to near Siderova, where she anchored for the night, not knowing how it fared with her two companions, who were astern and out of sight. After a very stormy night the morning broke with fine clear weather, and she proceeded, having now a good channel of five or six fathoms.

During the afternoon the *Offtzine* was joined by her companions, the *Malyguine* and *Bard*, and good progress was made. The following day saw us past Karaoul, and next day we stopped at Luko Protock to take in wood-fuel.

The *Graff Ignatieff* soon came up, and once more the flotilla was complete, and after wooding up, proceeded on the voyage. Strong currents and head-winds prevailing caused the lighters in tow to be a serious hindrance to our progress. However, without any further mishap worthy of notice, we arrived at last, on October 23rd, at the city of Yeneseisk, amidst a blinding snowstorm which cleared off shortly after our dropping anchor.

A sensational welcome awaited us. Thousands of people lined the shore and rent the air with

their hearty cheers, which were answered by the
tars on board our flotilla, and signal guns were
also fired.   In a short time a large steamer, the
Russia, owned by Mr. Guadaloff of Krasnoiarsk,
left the wharf laden with hundreds of passengers.
Sheering along the *Offtzine*, she made fast ; a
gangway plank was speedily slid on board, and
Lieutenant Dobrotvorscy was invited to meet the
Governor, the Mayor, and the Ispravnick, who with
others awaited him on the main deck.   A letter
of welcome was read and presented to him by the
Mayor, as well as a large iced cake surmounted
by a silver salt-cellar.   The national custom of
partaking of salt having been complied with, all
ceremony vanished.   Lieutenant Dobrotvorscy
returned, escorting the Mayor, Ispravnick, and
Bishop, who at once descended to the small
cabin, and others followed, until it was packed
to excess.   Meanwhile the decks were crowded
with people,—the principal merchants and ladies of
the city, who surrounded the other officers and me.

Hand-shaking and congratulations were the
order of the day, cheer after cheer arose from

the vicinity of the little cabin as toast after toast was quaffed, each cheer being answered to the echo by hundreds of voices from the *Russia*.

This lasted for some twenty minutes, until the functionaries all returned to the *Russia's* roomy promenade deck.

Casting loose, this splendid steamer started off, and again the air rang with plaudits from her crowded decks.

Another half hour found those on board the expeditionary vessels in a quiescent state, at leisure to realise the fact that now our long toil up river had ended, and that the first Russian fleet flying the Imperial flag had safely anchored in view of Siberian citizens. The yacht *Minusinsk* was noticed at the quay with her blue ensign flying, having arrived four days in advance, her cargo being all discharged.

And now the welcome on the shore was to commence. The following day a thanksgiving-service was held in the Cathedral, which is situated close to the shore, abreast of where the vessels lay at anchor. At 10 A.M. Lieutenant

Dobrotvorscy, with the officers and crews of his three ships, attended the solemn service, and the grand building was quickly filled to the porch by citizens of all classes, the young students of the girls' college being noticeable amongst them.

In the evening a grand banquet was prepared at the spacious club. All the principal officials of the city, including the Mayor, Ispravnick, and Bishop, as well as merchants, attended to do honour to their countrymen, who had braved the dangers of the icy seas in order to inaugurate a new era for their port. Congratulatory addresses were again read and presented to Lieutenant Dobrotvorscy. Toasts were drunk in honour of the Czar and of the promoters of the most important undertaking ever projected in Siberia ; and the Englishmen present were welcomed as brothers in the work now begun. I also came in for my share of the honours. On the naval men returning to the vessels in the small hours, a new surprise awaited them on the beach in the form of illuminations *à la Sibérienne*. Blue and red lights blazed forth from the high promenade

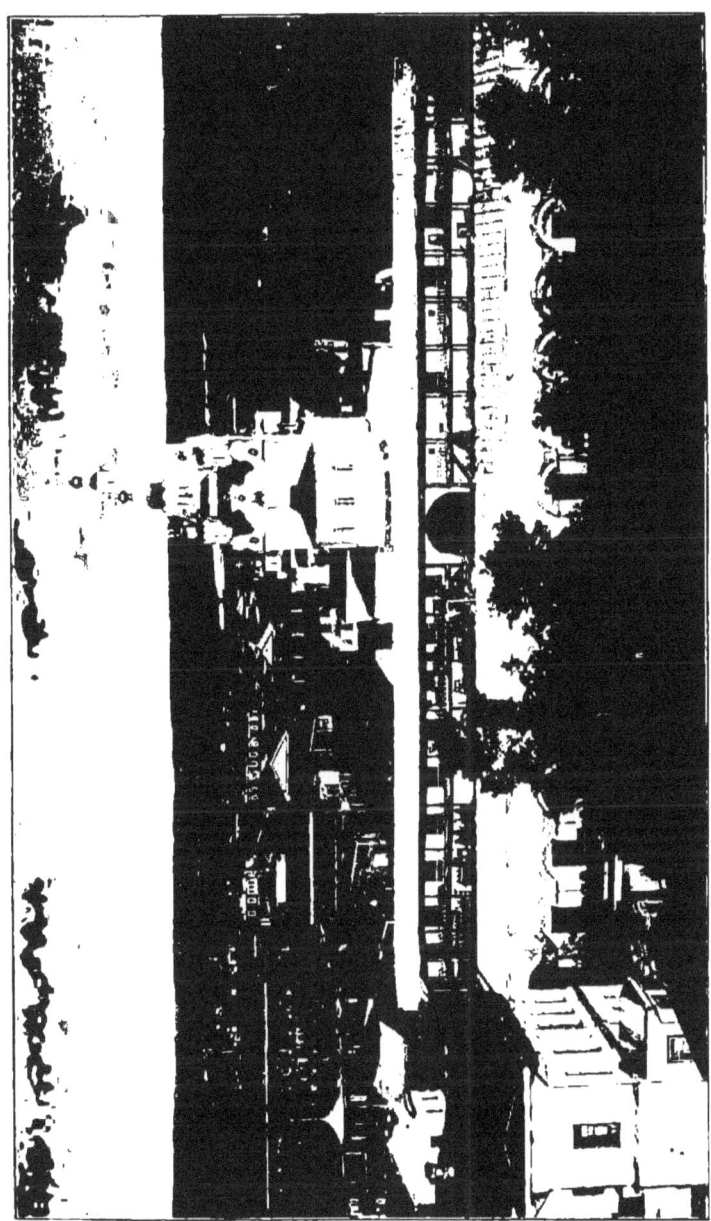

CATHEDRAL AND TOWN OF YENESEISK.

To face page 152.

overlooking the shore, and on the landing-place
an excellent band discoursed lively music until
the departure of Lieutenant Dobrotvorscy and
his officers in a steam-launch for their respective
vessels.

A few days afterwards a grand ball was given
at Mr. Chiromnick's handsome residence. All
the officers attended, and a most enjoyable time
was spent, the dancing not coming to a stop
until far into the morning hours.

The *Graff Ignatieff* started up the river at
once to Krasnoiarsk with some barges laden
with rails; and Lieutenant Dobrotvorscy in the
Malyguine, with the commanders of the *Bard* and
Scuratoff and myself, took a run up and down
river for many miles, to inspect small creeks suitable for laying-up places.

Several were found, and it was decided to lay
up the Russian vessels at Cawarova, some ten
miles below the town. The Mayor and citizens
protested, however, against this, and offered to
raise by subscription money sufficient to cut a
canal into the small creek which intersects the

city. The necessary amount was soon subscribed, and leave having been obtained by Lieutenant Dobrotvorscy from his Government to allow his vessels to remain there, it was decided to cut the channel at once, and men were set to work.

Meanwhile the ships were anchored close to the shore, where they will quietly freeze in for the winter, and in spring they will be moved into this canal or cutting, when it is flooded by the spring waters on the passing away of the large ice. Yeneseisk will thus be in possession of a good wet dock or port, which can be extended as may be needed in future years.

This speaks well for the goodwill and energy of the citizens, who must be prepared to encounter rivalry on the part of their neighbours at Krasnoiarsk, where the first rails which are destined to occupy a prominent place in history have been landed. It may be depended on, that the inhabitants of Krasnoiarsk will not rest contented merely by the Trans-Siberian railway passing through their city, but doubtless they will do their utmost to construct docks and other works, so as to tempt the sea-going steamers to winter there. The only impediments to Krasnoiarsk becoming a maritime port are the shallow channels and rapids which are met with on the way higher up river, necessitating the use of fast vessels drawing 5 feet or 6 feet, but those of 10 feet draught can reach this city.

At the end of October no ice had yet formed on the river, almost an unprecedented event, and indeed there were few signs of stern winter's approach, the weather being warm and open. This was probably caused by the hot atmospheric wave which passed over Europe generally, causing cases of sunstroke even in London.

The *Minusinsk* was laid up on the beach close to the entrance to the small creek, where she is in readiness to be hauled into the channel now being cut, as soon as the river rises in the spring of next year.

I rented a house, in which my crew have been comfortably located for the winter; and it was my intention to journey overland to Irkutsk and St. Petersburg on my way to London as soon as the roads were in a condition to admit of sleighing. At that time they were in a sad state of mud, which is a serious hindrance to travelling.

It has been already stated that the Government intends to despatch 1,000,000 poods (about 19,000 tons) of rails next summer, which means large business; and I may add that it is gratifying to know that Lieutenant Dobrotvorscy, the commander of the Russian Government expedition, has been promoted to the rank of Captain in the Imperial Navy, as he richly deserves this distinction for his unwearied exertions during this memorable voyage.

After a pleasant stay at Yeneseisk of two months or more, we prepared for our journey home overland, our party consisting of two engineers, two sailors, one cook, myself and my secretary. Three very strong (covered-in) sledges—with a hood on the after part—were purchased, and well strengthened and fitted with strong massive "out-riggers" or runners; our engineers had these and extra strengthenings, cross-bearers, etc., well bolted with strong iron stays from the upper body of the sledge. All the inside was lined out with thick hair-felt, strong mat-and-canvas aprons, fitted to pull up from the front of the sledge, and also pieces of canvas which drew up over the side to prevent snow entering whilst running at high speed, or when forcing our way through snow-drifts.

Added to this, our sailors were employed for several days making huge fur bags,—out of reindeer skins,—each bag large enough for all the occupants of each sledge to sleep in : No. 1 sledge, "*Black Bess*," containing myself and Secretary Byford ; No. 2 sledge, containing two engineers ; No. 3 sledge, with three occupants, two sailors and the cook.

The 19th of December saw us all in readiness for a start—noon the following day being the appointed time. During the whole of this day our farewell visitors swarmed in upon us to "chaï-peet" (take tea and cake) and speak adieus, etc. This lasted far into the night, the midnight hour having passed before our last kind visitors had said their farewells, when sundry finishing touches, etc., had to be made to our heavy packings.

At 9 A.M. the following morning the three sledges were drawn up to the back door in our spacious court-yard, and sledge-packing began in earnest, though little did our crew know about it. However, with plenty of sweet hay, our sundry sailor bags, portmanteaus, etc., were duly stowed away; a goodly stock of new loaves of bread, tins of preserved meats, soups, sugar, tea, coffee shared off to each sledge; then the large fur sleeping-bags laid over all, large feather pillows at the back, and all looked as comfortable and inviting to the *un*-wearied traveller as a large old-fashioned four-poster bed.

At noon precisely, three sets of hardy Siberian horses (nine in all) entered the yard. Soon they were yoked, and hasty farewells said to all our crew who were remaining behind, and rapid hand-shakes interchanged with several other visitors who again called to *see us off*, our old landlord getting the last shake as we past him standing at the open gates.

Out and on to the high road we dashed—our
snorting fiery steeds having it all their own way.
On through the wide main street of the city we
sped, our cheery sledge-bells loudly announcing
the (to us) important fact that another start had
been made for an overland journey to "Home,
sweet Home."

Turning to the left and passing the Town
Hall, we soon came on to the old Archinsk road
—a shorter way to Tomsk than the newer and
more frequented route by Krasnoiarsk. In a
little while our "yemshiks" (drivers) drew rein
to allow our followers to come up with us, and
then we found that several friends, including our
chief mate, Mr. Milne, and others of our crew
had accompanied us thus far for the purpose
of having a last farewell; this being over, off
we bounded on our course, while they returned
home. We three "troikers," with urging and
whooping yemshiks and willing steeds, settled
down steadily to the work before us.

The weather being delightfully fine and sunny,
we enjoyed a lovely clear afternoon, but as the

"shades of evening closed around us" King Frost asserted his rights and made himself keenly felt. We were not in possession of thermometers, but at a safe guess it must have registered 40° below zero of Fahr., nevertheless, being well wrapt in furs, riding was most enjoyable, and before we well knew where we were, our sledge dashed into the open gateway of the "star-roster's"[1] courtyard at the first station from Yeneseisk—now some twenty miles away.

We did not remain here to "chaï-peet," but having paid off drivers, fresh horses were quickly "put-to," and off we went again with the same invigorating whoops and yells of our fresh drivers, each "troiker" vieing with the other as to which should take precedence. This stimulating and praiseworthy effort on their part, though very enjoyable to witness, is nevertheless occasionally attended with danger — more especially to the charming little horses, who are very liable to plunge their feet into the open space of the out-rigger and the runner of the sledge which it is

[1] The head man of a village.

passing. This did actually occur on one of my former journeys, and I then made up my mind for no more " side by side " racing. Therefore, on this present occasion, we peremptorily commanded our driver to give way and to allow the sledge to drop astern ; and this rule was never swerved from during the whole of our journey. Though often attempts were made to infringe it, we at once compelled our driver to desist from them ; though when, as sailors would say, all were " end on " to each other, at a safe distance, we cheerfully permitted the anxious driver to head his rival by urging his horses to their best speed, but under no other circumstances could it be allowed.

At the second station we had the customary refreshment of " chaï-peet," with boiled fresh eggs and delicious cream, for which we paid twenty kopeks, 6d. On we sped, night and day, from village to village, passing through the busy town of Archinsk the second day, and arriving at Tomsk city by midnight on the 24th December. There we were very glad to turn in to the best hotel of this large and busy city, in order to thaw ourselves,

M

for the cold was so intense that everything in our sledges, fur sleeping-bags included, were frozen solid. Two spacious rooms with large heating stoves were allotted to our private use, and, once in an atmosphere of some 70° plus Fahr., we soon discussed a hasty cup of refreshing tea, and stretched our weary limbs on good spring mattresses to thaw. At such a time as this, one of the most trying punishments for the traveller is to unpack his sledge, everything having to be brought indoors to be thawed. The only trial to be in any way compared to it is the re-packing the sledge again : this, when done in the more genial warmth of daytime, is quite painful enough, but when during the cold midnight hours, loading or more especially *unloading*, after a bitter cold ride of several days, the work is torture indeed.

At Tomsk we stayed and had our Christmas Day. It not being the time for the Russian festival—theirs being twelve days later—we were in comparative quietness. We had a good hearty dinner of four or five courses *à la Sibérienne*, and cakes, etc., with coffee, afterwards. A good substantial supper followed, and by midnight one and all declared themselves once more well thawed and quite equal to, and eager for, the road. Horses were again ordered, sledges packed, and hearty toast after toast drunk to the health and well-being of " old and young folks at home " from the " cup that cheers but not inebriates." Having paid due homage to our steaming " samovar," and settled all scores with our accommodating host, we again tumble into our fur bags, and by the silvery light of a full moon we wend our silent way through the wide streets of this large city. Arriving at the boundary-gate our bells are once more loosened,[1] and again we bound along over the snow-white road at a rattling pace, everything literally sparkling with light and sledge-bells ringing forth their merry peals, all tending to inspire the traveller with feelings of joy and peace.

New Year's Day found us arrived in safety at the busy city of Omsk, where we once more had

[1] All bells are forbidden to be loose whilst passing through large towns.

to go through the thawing process — this time
it required three days to accomplish. We had
three large rooms allotted to us .at the Hotel
Moscow, and after seeing the New Year well
in we again took the road, to find the cold keener
than ever. For my own part, although I have
travelled overland six times, yet I never experienced such piercing cold. Had we neglected
supplying ourselves with fur bags, we should
certainly not have been able to bear it. As it
was, my face, for the first time in all my many
thousands of miles of sledging, was "frost-bitten."
However, we kept pegging away; our crew,
unused to such refrigerating experiences, sturdily
made up their minds not to be beaten, with the result
that Wednesday the 4th January saw us in a semi-
frozen state entering the busy town of Kurgan.

The morning was bright and sunny, with intense
cold, when to our utter amazement we suddenly
overtook the most extraordinary caravan or rather
cavalcade that it has ever been our lot to see,—a
number of huge camels, some thirty or more, each
animal drawing a large sledge laden with heavy

machinery. An immense sack of thick hair-felt enveloped each beast from stem to stern, coming down from the top of its unsightly hump to the lower part of its body or middle of its lanky legs. To see such animals, denizens of warm climates, quietly stalking along, their bare soft feet all exposed to the sharp and cutting ice of the hard roads, icicles pendant from their highly elevated nostrils, was curious indeed. Each camel was attended by its quiet and quaint-looking Tartar or Mongolian leader, walking demurely by the side of the outlandish-looking animal, making a picture of never-to-be-forgotten patience and endurance. Surely no hot sands of the desert can ever produce the pain and suffering which these patient creatures were now called upon to endure; yet they seemed to do, indeed were doing, their work as quietly and unconcerned as though in their own warmer climate of the southern steppes, having probably drawn those heavily-laden sledges many hundreds of miles. It was hard to decide which was most deserving of wonder and praise—the patient and weird-looking Mongolian leader or the ungainly brute that he led. It was decidedly the most unique exhibition it has ever been my lot to see.

By noon we had crossed the first section of the overland route of railway that has as yet reached these far limits of Russia. We had been told at Omsk that the railway was made as far as Kurgan, but we found it was finished some twenty miles farther, and well finished too. Soon we entered the town and located ourselves at the Post-House, hoping to leave by rail during the same evening, and thus to bid farewell to all our sufferings by cold and sledge-bumping. We disposed of our three strong sledges for a moiety of what they had cost us, and then took a town single sledge to our railway station, situated some two miles outside the town. Here we found none of the clerks or ordinary officials able to converse in English, or indeed able to give us the least information, but at last they advised us to call upon the manager and chief constructor, a Mr. Stuckinbergh.

Arrived at his domicile we were ushered into

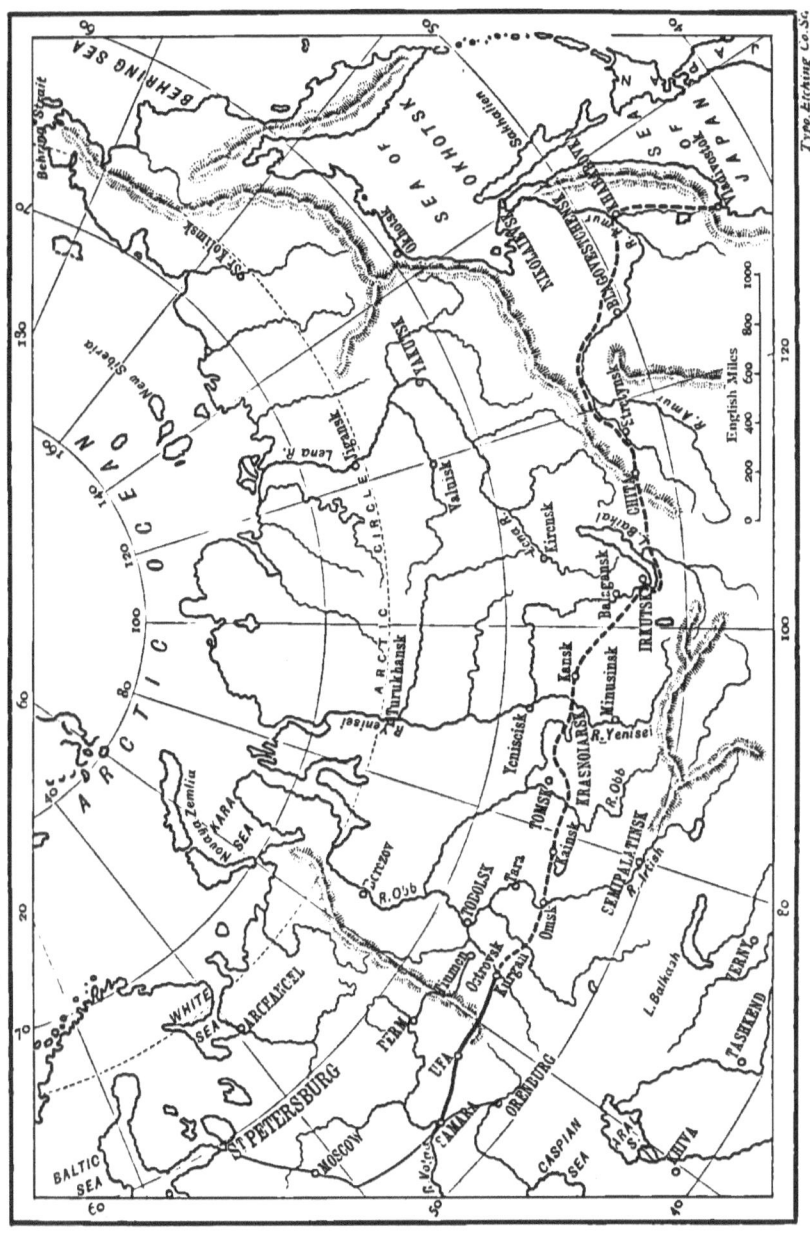

Route of the Great Siberian Railway.

Type-Etching Co. Sc.

To face page 166.

his presence, to find him as reticent as his officials, but on our explaining to him that we were Britishers he hastily requested me to follow him into his spacious drawing - room, informing me as he led the way that Madam S. "Gabareet pa roosky e po anglesky." Soon this assurance was verified by the appearance of a charming lady, who accosted me fluently in my mother tongue. The genial manager informed me through this medium that, there being no passenger carriages, we should have to await the arrival of one from Cheliabinsk, the only place that such carriages were allowed to run to. This would require at least two days. Meanwhile, should we not be able to secure one by this means, he was prepared to give us his own private house-carriage or waggon that he used when on his journeys along the lines. Having spent a pleasant hour or more, we retired to the Post-House, partook of a hearty meal, and turned in for the night.

The next day, no carriage having been forwarded from Cheliabinsk, we were informed by

the kind and gracious railway manager that it
was his intention to send us forward with his
own carriage, which would be attached to the train
leaving at 10 P.M.   Meanwhile he placed an
empty lock-up covered-in waggon at our disposal
for transmitting our heavy luggage.   At the time
appointed we started under the most comfortable circumstances on our free *unpaid* journey
to Cheliabinsk ; there were not only soft beds
but even a good "samovar" and cooking stove.
With these improved conditions we sped along
at a safe pace of some thirty miles per hour,
which speed is seldom increased.   Nevertheless
it does not ensure from severe accidents occasionally happening.   About 4 A.M. the following
morning we were aware that, for some unex-
plained reason, our train was at a stand-still,
and this continued up to 8 A.M.   We heard
sundry whistlings and shunting to and fro of
our engine.   At last we descried it passing our
train with a smashed-up locomotive in tow ; then
we realised that an accident had occurred.   On
inquiry we found it had nothing to do with

the fortunes of our train, further than a lengthy
detention of many hours ere the line could be
cleared was involved, but that two ballast trains had
collided going in opposite directions, smashing both
engines and several waggons, and some men, including engineers and stokers, being severely injured.
This was confirmed by three poor fellows being
transferred to the comforts of our special carriage.
We afterwards learnt that this accident was
entirely owing to the effects of the festive season;
we were assured that as a rule few or no
accidents occur.

The next day we arrived safely at Cheliabinsk,
where we found a large and handsome station,
built of granite, and all the other large out-
buildings, such as railway engine sheds, maga-
zines, store-houses, also built in a massive manner
of the same material; a spacious restaurant
adorned the handsome hall of the station; everything, indeed, was in a highly finished condition.
Many trains of passengers and goods were awaiting departure—excellent carriages, all well heated
with stoves, and even the third class replete

with all necessary conveniences for long journeys, and exceedingly comfortable.

Here we booked to Toula, thence to Libau and the historical city of Smolensk. At Libau I succeeded in obtaining a passage for my sailors direct to London in a steamer belonging to Copenhagen.

Having despatched my men, I took train at once for St. Petersburg, where I found Mr. Popham awaiting me at the Hotel d'Angleterre. During our stay of a few weeks we had the honour of interviewing the Minister of Finance, Minister of Marine, Minister of Ways of Communication, and others, also the Committee for the Construction of the Siberian Railway, with whom we had several earnest consultations in meetings assembled to organise the work for the sea-route. All this resulted in a decision not to prosecute the work by the sea-route for at least a while, the Railway Committee being under the impression that it would prove more costly than completing only the overland route. However, this important project has not yet been finally

abandoned. Further discussions are to take place
on the arrival of Captain Dobrotvorscy from
Yeneseisk, when it is to be hoped that he,
together with the Minister of Marine (who is
most anxious to develop the over-sea trade), will
be able to convince the Board not merely of
the feasibility of this sea-route, but also the
great importance it will have in the future success
and rapid development of this " Land of Goshen."
By working in conjunction with the mighty
Trans-Siberian system of railway, it would relieve
it of the enormous amount of heavy transit, such
as raw produce from Siberia, and cumbersome
manufactures, machinery, etc., from Europe —
articles that will finally prove too bulky and
plentiful for the railway to carry at a profit.
And it does not require a prophet to foresee
the fact that without such a free outlet for her
produce as "this northern sea-route," it will be
of small use for the Russian Government to
establish such excellent means of internal communication as this splendid railway, to pour into
central and eastern Siberia large numbers of

colonists, as it is their intention to do, merely to raise up that land by agriculture, mining, etc., without taking advantage of the sea-route that is now open to them.

Grand as the results of the " Trans-Siberian Railway " will most assuredly be, yet it must be borne in mind that it can never transmit and relieve the country of one third or fourth the produce that can and will assuredly be the outcome of her augumented inhabitants.

I append to this brief description of my overland journey an extract taken from a book on the Industries of Russia,[1] and dealing with Siberia, prepared for the World's Columbian Exposition, which enables one to realise the immensity and great importance of the " Trans-Siberian Railway " when once completed.

In conclusion, let us hope that—the Russian Government having now proved to their own satisfaction and to the world at large that commercial relations can, and therefore ought to, be held with her Siberian territories by aid

[1] See Appendix A.

of the *sea-route*, making use of those noble rivers Yenesei and Obi that would otherwise be idle — we may now see such a grand work vigorously prosecuted and encouraged for this next season and all future time, by the Russian Government issuing orders for the conveyance by sea of rails and goods of all kinds required for the construction of their great railway, and for the general welfare of "Siberia in Asia."

CHAPTER XI

IT will be borne in mind that this heroic man with his small band of followers—in his arctic-built steamer *Fram*—reached the port of Khaba-rova or "St. Nicholas," in the Pet Straits, at the entrance to the Kara Sea, in safety about the middle of August last. Here he received on board his sledge-dogs, which had been brought overland from Obdorsk on the Obi by a mes-senger, who happened to be the very same man who served under me in the *Labrador* during our 1888 expedition, and who accompanied young Victor Morier overland to Obdorsk from Khaba-rova. To this young man Nansen delivered letters and despatches, etc., for home, all of which arrived safely to hand during this winter.

In an effort mentally to follow up the course pursued and trace the likely whereabouts of this gallant leader, it will be as well to commence our imaginary voyage from the scene of this last place, Khabarova, from where positive news has come to hand.

Nansen must have found the Kara Sea well free of ice, always presuming that he kept his vessel in the spacious open water traversed by our vessels, and never attempting to take the pack-ice, which occupied only the central portion of the Kara Sea. We may therefore take it for granted that the *Fram* has succeeded in arriving safely in the vicinity of the Dickson-Haven group of islands, at the outer or north-west extremity of the entrance to the Gulf of Yenesei — our farthest point before turning our vessels south to run up that mighty stream.

It was here that we found the heavy pack-ice rather close on to the land, leading away to the north-west. This mass of pack-ice left so soon as we turned south, but Nansen, some days previous to our arrival, would, on the contrary, be obliged to close in with this ice and work his way along the north-west coast. How he may have fared is mere conjecture, though I am under the impression that this ice was not tight on to the coast, in which case we must suppose that they would soon be able to reach the northernmost point or headland of Asia, Cape " Chelyuskin," the Ultima Thule or Cape " Tabin " of the Ancients.

Arriving at this interesting locality, it would then become a serious question to Nansen as to what might be the best course for him to pursue. Should the open water be extensive and lead far north, it would be a severe temptation for him to push direct " Northward - Ho." And in such an event (which I sincerely hope may have occurred) we may have no further news of the gallant ship and her heroic crew until they emerge by way of Greenland, Spitzbergen, or Franz Josef Land, or beat a retreat by way of Novaia Zemlia or the shores of the Asiatic mainland. Should they be driven on to the eastern or northern coast of Franz Josef

Land (in a similar manner to the Austrian Expedition ship *Tegethoff*, under the command of
that most excellent and daring man, the late
Lieutenant Weyprecht), let us hope that the
Jackson party, now preparing to leave our shores
for an overland trip to the North Pole by that
route, may fall in with and so join, if not succour
and rescue, the brave Norwegians.

Should, however, the pack-ice be in close
proximity to the Asiatic shore after passing
round Cape Chelyuskin, then Nansen will be
obliged to shape his course along the land. In
this case we ought in a short time, or at latest
during this summer, to hear of them having called
in at the depôt of the "Olenek" River, where
more dogs are now awaiting their arrival. If it
turns out that the Expedition has not touched at
the depôt, we must presume that circumstances
have caused them to proceed northward, or on
to the New Siberian Islands, where, on the
northernmost island, stores were deposited last
year by that unwearied traveller Baron Toll,
who was sent out by the Russian Government,

N

and lately returned to St. Petersburg direct from that locality.

I enjoyed several pleasant conversations with the Baron and his lieutenant during their short sojourn at Yeneseisk as he was on his way home in December last, this being the second journey the Baron has made to those desolate and far regions of the north, mostly on foot, accompanied by natives and dog-sledges.

Should Nansen reach this spot — the New Siberian Islands — we may hear nothing more of them until some one happens to go there for the purpose of ascertaining whether or not the Expedition has called at the Islands. Probably the gallant Baron may contemplate another and third visit to his favourite resort this summer for this purpose. If so, we may possibly have word and receive despatches from Nansen during the ensuing winter.

But, whether we do or do not hear of those brave men, of this we may be assured, that, providing no accident has occurred to their vessel, they will, during next summer, be hard

at work testing the (to them) all-important question : Is there a road to or round by the North
Pole by proceeding north? If they have pushed
to the north, either last summer or during this
coming season, we may be sure of one thing,
that the heroic band will for a certainty experience the serious if not awful risk of being
beset in the dread pack-ice, in the same manner
as was the *Jeannette*, of the ill-fated American
Expedition, a few years ago.   Should this be
the case, the probability (amounting to almost a
certainty) is that the vessel, strong though she
be, will never return by the same route they
have pursued, seeing that the oceanic currents
are constantly flowing northward and over
towards the North Pole, and they will, *nolens
volens*, take them, and the pack-ice which holds
them in its vice-like grasp, onward towards the
goal of their brave hearts' desire.   The only thing
that can happen to prevent their arrival will
be new lands ; these will almost certainly arrest
their further progress, and probably land their
vessel, and the ice on which she may possibly

be cradled, high and dry on shore. As happened with the Austrians, in this case it will become imperative to abandon the *Fram*, and the crew will make their escape by retreating, homewards or onwards by the Pole or its vicinity. In such an extremity I feel sure that the watchword of that heroic leader and his brave band will be *Excelsior !*

This being so, let us hope on that we shall actually hear of their safe arrival, after many hardships and dangers, at the shores of North Greenland, where, in such a happy event, they may meet with the interesting American Expedition, now prosecuting researches in those unknown quarters, under the leadership of Lieutenant Peary. What a delightful episode and glorious conclusion this would prove !

Finally, should the little vessel succumb to the severe pressure and rough handling of the pack-ice in the Siberian seas, then we ought to hear of Nansen's arrival by way of the Asiatic or Siberian coast, provided he can but succeed in making good a safe landing, as we have

been assured that the many natives who constantly roam those shores have been warned to
assist and report any Europeans or civilised men
happening to need their assistance ; indeed, the
Russian Government seem to have left nothing
undone in order to assist these heroes, whether
they be in trouble or not.   For our part, though
the chances may seem remote, we live in hopes
of again hearing of that gallant crew.   And
should it so happen that years roll by and no
news come from that silent land of the eternal
frost-king, we may hope to see, not merely one,
but many a search party or expedition going
forth with the determination to do daring deeds
for the rescue of those who have so nobly done
their duty to their country and the world at
large.   I feel sure there are many brave men
who will gladly volunteer to undertake such a
noble and sacred work, and it will only need
the response of those who have the means, to
enable those who have the heart to search for
the lost ones far away.   But I hope that this
may not be found necessary, and trust that,

before many years are past we may hear of
Nansen's safe arrival home, whether *viâ* the
North Pole or not.

Of one thing the gallant expedition may be
very sure, they have the world's good wishes for
their entire success.

*A Letter from Frederick G. Jackson on his pro-
posed Polar Expedition.*

Photograph by Maull and Fox.   187a Piccadilly, London.

FREDERICK G. JACKSON.

To face page 185.

CHAPTER XII

14th March 1894.

DEAR MISS PEEL—It is with much pleasure that
I comply with your request to give you an outline of the plans which I hope to carry out on my
Franz Josef Land Expedition this summer, more
especially as you have so identified yourself with
matters Polar in being one of the only two ladies
who have ever traversed the icy waters of the
Kara Sea in the recent Yenesei Expedition, with
which Expedition I had the privilege of going as
far as the Yugor Straits.

It would, perhaps, be better to begin by stating
my reasons for entering on this Expedition.

First of all, I am extremely desirous of seeing
the British once more taking that foremost place

in arctic discovery which in past times they so
easily held, and I felt that the absence of our
countrymen in the present striving for the Pole
is most certainly not in accordance with the
past.

My second reason lies in the fact that I have
been able to choose a route which, in my opinion
and in that of our leading arctic authorities, is
the one which holds out the greatest probability
of reaching a high latitude. In Franz Josef
Land, as far as one knows, and can gather, there
exists a practicable avenue as far north as the
highest latitude yet attained, and holding out
the probability of leading even farther north.

My plans, as far as I have made them at the
present date, are briefly as follows : Embarking
in a strong vessel suitable for the arctic regions,
and having steam power, we sail from the
Thames towards the end of July next, and shall
probably touch at Archangel and Khabarova
in order to pick up, at the former place, a few
stores and ponies, and at the latter my dogs
and probably a few Samoyedes. We then push

north on about the 50th east meridian, the lay of the ice of course deciding.

Hoping to safely negotiate the eighty—more or less—miles of ice south of Franz Josef Land, we shall reach the shores of that country, we trust, early in September, and after securing the ship in a safe harbour, we shall immediately land all our stores and provisions, and build a strong house in which we shall pass the first winter, and in building which we shall be helped by the ship's crew. When this has been done and things made snug, the ship will make her departure, and I trust reach England safely in October.

When the ship has sailed, our party will consist of about nine persons (if I take Samoyedes). We shall prepare for the rapidly on-coming winter, and shall stock our larder with everything we can shoot. Our time for doing this with the comfort which the presence of the sun will add, will be short, for towards the end of October we shall lose the sun.

My great object during the winter, I need

hardly say, will be to keep up the spirits of the party, and we shall do this by indulging in all active exercises possible under the circumstances.

In the following spring, on the return of the sun, we shall push north, making depôts of food every thirty or forty miles, our route being up Austria Sound (aided in drawing our sledges by our dogs and Russian ponies), at all events as far as Cape Higely.

Past that point our route is shrouded in a certain amount of uncertainty, but our next objective will be Petermannland, which Payer has distinctly stated to extend north of Aa, 83° N.L.

I am in great hopes that Petermannland may extend directly north and for a considerable distance. Should this not be the case, and oceanic ice lie in our path, our task in pushing north will be one of great difficulty, as it goes without saying that depôts cannot be established upon sea-ice, which will almost certainly be hummocky and in motion.

Although we are few in number we shall

have among us men of scientific training and experience, so that we may bring back a complete series of observations and collections, and contribute, I hope, something of interest to physical and natural science.

It is difficult to say much at this rather early stage about the exact nature of the equipment, but I have made up my mind to model my fur clothing on that of the Samoyede people, the shape and character of which are, in my opinion, most suitable. The sledges will be of the one-man type (Norwegian pattern), but with certain additions and alterations suggested to me by my experiences during my last expedition. On our northward march we shall also take boats of a special type and make.

Of course we shall have with us tinned foods of considerable variety, but as long as we can get fresh meat we shall not use these much. The object will be to reduce the impedimenta as much as possible, and to carry with us only the actual necessaries for existence and for scientific work. We may be two years away, or we may

be four, but whether the time be short or long, I
hope the results of the Expedition will be such
as to reflect credit not only upon those who have
taken part in it but upon the country for whose
fame they make the effort.—Yours sincerely,

FREDERICK G. JACKSON.

APPENDICES

APPENDIX A (see p. 172)

THE wide expanse and sparse population of Siberia, combined with historical destiny, have prevented its being enriched with regular overland means of communication, which could only have been accomplished at the expense of a vast amount of labour and capital. Nature has, on the other hand, richly endowed this country with water communication, washed on the north and east by the waters of the Arctic and Pacific Oceans. It is at the same time intersected for thousands of versts by large rivers connecting these oceans with western China, and in general with central Asia. Thanks to these rivers, whose basins cover several million square versts, in summer time it is possible to communicate with far distant regions. This was the route

o

taken by the conquerors of Siberia and the settlers who followed them, coming from the west, but of late years communication has been kept up with Siberia by sea from the north and from the east. Unfortunately the insufficiency of the coast development on the one hand, and the severe climate of the arctic zone on the other hand, prevent the sea navigation from reaching that degree of development which would be possible under more favourable conditions. This same severity of climate, and the prolonged period during which the rivers are in consequence frozen, considerably hinders navigation on the principal Siberian rivers which fall into the Arctic Ocean. The most important rivers of Siberia, the Obi, Yenesei, and Lena, flow from south to north, and are for the greater part of their course navigable. Only one river, the Amour, flows to the east, and, at the junction with the Sungara, turns northwards and falls into the Pacific Ocean.

The establishment of steam communication with the Far East, undertaken in 1870 by the

Russian Steam Navigation and Trade Company, did not possess any serious commercial importance. This undertaking also assumed large dimensions only from the moment when the Volunteer Fleet established regular communication between Odessa and Vladivostok, calling at several Chinese ports on the way. This institution, called into existence in 1878 during the last eastern war, with the object of performing the duty of cruisers in war time and having commercial objects in time of peace, certainly gave a great impulse to the connecting of European Russia with the Far East, and strengthening the influence of Russia in the waters of the Pacific Ocean. The Volunteer Fleet, whose ships are completely adapted to long ocean voyages, is every year increasing its activity in the conveyance of passengers and goods from the ports of the Black Sea to Vladivostok, barely satisfying the demands made upon it. Thanks to its activity, eastern Siberia now receives a mass of necessary articles from European Russia and not from abroad, and European

Russia gets Chinese tea much cheaper than by land.

In the way of land communication but one road passes through Siberia at all deserving attention, this being the so-called Great Siberian Tract, joining Moscow with Irkutsk, or more exactly with Kiakhta. Within the actual limits of Siberia it commences at Tiumen and passes through Yalutorovsk, Ishim, Tiukalinsk, Kainsk, Kolyvan, Tomsk, Marinsk, Achinsk, Krasnoiarsk, Nizhneoudinsk. In this direction also took place the principal colonisation of Siberia. Hence one road goes to Kiakhta and continues farther into the Celestial Empire, while another goes to Baikal, upon which in summer there is steam communication, and in winter by sledge. There is also a road round Baikal passing through an extremely irregular country. Further on, the post road from Verkneoudinsk to Stretensk traverses very difficult places, where sometimes no snow whatever falls, in consequence of which, in winter, the driver is not seldom obliged here to carry his sledge on a cart, or, on the other hand, to put the cart on runners. The thinness of the population in the country along this road, inhabited mainly by vagrants, makes the conveyance of freights extremely difficult and expensive. From this point to Khabarovka the road follows the Amour, but few make use of it. In summer people prefer to take advantage of the water communication. In winter they travel in sledges over the ice, and only the break up of the ice or some other hard necessity forces them to turn to the natural earth road. The further communication with the terminal points of Siberia, Nikolaevsk, and Vladivostok, is carried on in summer by water and in winter on the ice. In autumn and spring almost all communication is stopped here.

After the annexation of the extensive Amour and littoral territories and of the Ussuri region, the want was felt of good ways of communication, on the one hand, in order to keep possession of them, and, on the other, in order to attract settlers and form new centres of population. In consequence of this a series of schemes

appeared for the construction of new roads in
Siberia, and Count Mouraviev-Amourski himself
was almost the first who conceived the idea of a
railway in this country.   Finally, by an Imperial
rescript given the 17th of March 1891, in the
name of His Imperial Highness the Tsarevitch,
the question of the construction of the Great
Siberian Railway was finally and irrevocably
decided in the affirmative.   The gracious will
of His Majesty the Emperor clearly expressed in
this rescript put an end to many years of hesitation and doubt as to the accomplishment of the
said great undertaking, and now the Government
has taken all the necessary measures for the most
successful realisation possible of this good conception, which has a perfect right to take one of
the first places among the most extensive and
important enterprises of the expiring century, not
only in this country but in the whole world.

The total length of the Siberian Railway, from
Cheliabinsk to Vladivostok along the main line is
7063 versts, and 7112 versts including branch
lines to the principal rivers intersecting the main

road. The whole line across Siberia will, therefore, be terminated in twelve years, counting from
1893. The Great Siberian Railway lies in the
mean geographical latitudes, and, as regards
climate and soil, possesses all the qualities favourable to the development of agriculture, rural
economy, and the industries connected with them.
It is worthy of attention also that, according to
the propitious choice of the direction of the
Great Siberian Railroad, which connects the
fertile lands of western Siberia and the distant
region of Ussuri, it also embraces the richest
deposits of the noble metals. It cannot be disputed that the line, when once laid, will give a
powerful impetus to the whole economical development of the country, and will call into
existence many new branches of industrial
activity.

Turning to the more intimate influence of the
Great Railroad upon the various features of
industrial and economic life in Siberia, it is
evident that the chosen route traverses the rich
Ishimsk, Barabinsk, and Kulundinsk steppes,

which have always been renowned for their fertility, and serve as a granary for Siberia.

Of late years, in many parts of European Russia, the increase of population from natural causes has brought about an excess of the labouring contingent, and the systematic increase of the number of peasants insufficiently provided with land, due to this fact, has already for some time past attracted the attention of the Government. For these reasons free Government lands in the mentioned localities are granted to settlers, and for their benefit a cheap rate has been fixed for conveying them by rail; in some cases they receive loans of money from the Government, and certain other privileges are granted to them in order to assist them in the difficulty of emigrating and of acquiring new household goods. Thus the Great Siberian Railway, animating the uninhabited fertile lands, ruled by the Governor - General of the steppes, and opening up an extensive market for the sale of all products of the earth, would at the same time assist the successful solution of one of the most difficult problems of the State, namely, the definite organisation of the economical condi- tion of the peasants badly provided with land in the internal Governments of European Russia. The mineral wealth and mining industry of Siberia shows how enormous are the riches in the bowels of the country, and what little use has been made of them up to the present time. Iron and coal, the two great factors of industrial de- velopment, are found nearly over all Siberia, and in very rich veins. The Great Siberian Railway will also have a great influence upon gold mining, as well as upon the extension of local trade, which beyond a doubt will be most considerable, many articles or raw materials, for which there is at present no local demand, will find a ready sale at more distant markets.

In order to grasp the whole extent of the actual importance of the Great Siberian Railway for Russian trade, we must bear in mind the fact that uninterrupted railroad communication will be established between Europe and the Pacific and the Far East. Thus the Siberian Railway opens

a new route and new horizons for universal as
well as for Russian trade ; it will be of immense
economic importance to Russia, and will give a
great impulse to Russian industry ; it will con-
nect 400 million Chinese and 35 million Japanese
with Europe through Russia.   The strenuous
endeavours made by Germany to gain possession
of the markets of the Pacific, and the efforts
which have been made to complete the Panama
Canal, visibly show that the economic struggle
already commenced will end on the Pacific
Ocean.   The Canadian railroad has now appro-
priated part of the freight of silk, tea, and furs
which previously reached Europe through the
Suez.   Undoubtedly part of these goods will
pass through Russia, as the journey from Europe
through Vladivostok to Shanghai will be made
in eighteen or twenty days, instead of forty-
five through Suez, or thirty - five days at
present by the Canadian Railway.   The
Siberian line will therefore not only have the
effect of increasing the importance of Russia
in the universal markets, but new sources of

national wealth will abundantly open around her.

There is no occasion to dwell upon the political importance of the Great Siberian Railway. Its significance is clear from the fact that when the line is completed Russia will not only nominally, but actually occupy that position in the east of Asia which it holds among its friends and enemies in Europe.

APPENDIX B

Monday, August 7, 1893.

3 P.M.—Ran into Vardoe Harbour, and moored with two anchors ahead and stern to buoys.

Log showed 108 miles.   Barometer 29.86.   Thermometer 57.

Wind westerly, moderate.

Later.—A strong north-west gale, with heavy rain.

Friday, August 11.

Heavy rain till 7 A.M.

Taking coals and water on board, and sending provisions to *Orestes* and *Minusinsk.*

Bar. 29.80.   Therm. 54.

Thursday, August 17.

A moderate west to north-west breeze and showery.

The Russian vessels came in at 8.30 A.M.

Bar. at 2 P.M. 29.72.   Therm. 52.

Later.—Wind freshening.

Tuesday, August 22.

Light south-east breeze and hazy.

The Russian vessels and *Minusinsk* went at 8 A.M.

Bar. 30.   Therm. 53.

Wednesday, August 23.

4 A.M.—Unmoored and steamed to sea.

5.10 A.M.—Set log and course east by south. Wind fresh, south-east by east.   Set fore and aft sails.

Bar. 30.2.   Therm. 50.

Noon.—Wind increasing.

4 P.M.—Fog and rain.   Hauled in light sails.

5 P.M.—Hauled in jib.

Thursday, August 24.

A fresh breeze from south-east by east, and hazy.

Bar. 30.4.   Therm. 52.

Log showed 126 miles.

4.30 P.M.—*Orestes* took us in tow.

Friday, August 25.

A fresh easterly breeze, with overcast sky.   Set fore and aft sails.

Log showed 174 miles at noon.

Latitude at noon 70.59.   Longitude 48.9 E.

Saturday, August 26.

Foggy, rain and sleet first part of day.

7 A.M.—Saw some ice, and kept round south end of it.

Bar. 29.64.   Therm. 42.

Latitude 70.11.   Longitude 55.52.

10 P.M.—*Orestes* hove off our tow-rope.

Sunday, August 27.

8 A.M.—Anchored at mouth of Yugor Straits. The three Russian vessels lying here and a sloop-of-war.

1 P.M.—Weighed anchor and steamed through the Straits; found no ice.

Came back and dropped anchor to wait for *Minusinsk*.

Bar. 29.84.   Therm. 41.

Tuesday, August 29.

5 A.M. — Weighed anchor and proceeded under steam.

A few pieces of ice coming through the Straits.

8.20 A.M. — Anchored off Khabarova. Put the launch and two dinghies out and started to take in fresh water.

1.30 P.M.—Took the boats on board, weighed anchor and proceeded, the *Orestes* towing the *Minusinsk*.

5 P.M.—Came to some loose ice; going slow all night; thick fog.

10 P.M.—Got into open water.

Wednesday, August 30.

Started full speed at daylight.

8 A.M.—Had to stop for the Russian vessels.

10 A.M.—Set all sail and stopped engines.

11 P.M.—Mr. Popham shot two walrus ; saw a great many on the ice and in the water.

Thursday, August 31.

Latitude 72.00.   Longitude 67.51.

Bar. 29.86.   Therm. 43.

Sighted the Yalmal Land.

Keeping the lead going 15 fathoms.   10 P.M. 13 fathoms ; hauled up north by west.

Friday, September 1.

At 4 A.M. altered course to north-east by north, 12 fathoms, log showed 95 miles.

Latitude 73.56 N.   Longitude 70.37 E.

Saturday, September 2.

5.30 P.M.—Dickson's Haven, north-east, 3 miles.

11.30 P.M.—Came to anchor on the north side in 10 fathoms.

Sunday, September 3.

3.30 A.M.—Weighed anchor and proceeded ; set all sail.

10 A.M.—Hauled in sails ; going dead slow ; using lead ; 5 fathoms.

Steering south-east, then east by south ; water deepening to 7 fathoms.

10.30 P.M.—Came to anchor at Golchika.

Monday, September 4.

Bar. 29.46.   Therm. 50.

Strong breeze from westward and passing showers of hail.

Lifted anchor and shifted off shore, and moored with 45 fathoms each way.

Monday, September 11.

Light south-east wind and clear.   All hands at the *Orestes*.   The *Minusinsk* went up the river to Yeneseisk at 2 P.M.

7 P.M.—The wind freshening.   Went up the river with steam launch.

Wednesday, September 13.

A fresh gale from south-west, with fog and rain.

Two lighters broke adrift from the *Orestes* and went on shore at 5 A.M.

Thursday, September 14.

6 A.M.—Weighed anchors and steered for a few miles up the river.   The wind veered to south and freshened to a gale with snow.   Ran back, and moored with 75 and 80 fathoms.

Barometer fell from 29.40 to 28.80.

Noon.—Less wind.

4 P.M.—The wind veered to north-west, and freshened to a strong gale. Barometer commenced to rise.

10 P.M.—Bar. 29.22. Therm. 43.

Saturday, September 16.

A strong southerly gale, with fog and rain.

At 6 A.M.—The anchors commenced to drag. Started engines.

7.30 A.M.—Weighed anchors, and steamed across to the west side of the river, and came to anchor in $7\frac{1}{2}$ fathoms.

Bar. 29.8. Therm. 44.

Monday, September 18.

A fresh southerly breeze and cloudy.

6 A.M.—Got under way and steamed up river a few miles ; much sea and thick fog at times.

Mr. Popham and Mr. James went shooting, and secured ten brace of ptarmigan.

Wednesday, September 20.

4 A.M.—Weighed anchor, and proceeded down the river.

Bar. 29.20. Therm. 38.

7 A.M.—The *Orestes* took us in tow.

Thursday, September 21.

A strong westerly breeze, clear, with frequent thick showers of snow.

P

Going along the south edge of the ice in tow by the *Orestes*.

Latitude 73.39.   Longitude 76.29.

Bar. 29.40.   Therm. 38.

Sunday, September 24.

A fresh south-south-east breeze, with thick fog.   Sea smooth.

6 A.M.—Cleared.   Had to haul out south-south-east for ice.

Noon.—Thick fog.   Steaming through loose ice towards the land.

8 P.M.—Cleared a little, and saw land.

9 P.M.—Anchored in 14 fathoms.

Latitude 70.18 N.   Longitude 62.14.

Bar. 29.70.   Therm. 45.

Monday, September 25.

5.30 A.M.—Weighed anchor, and proceeded along the land.

Noon.—Thick fog ; ship going dead slow ; keeping lead going.

Grounded off Waigatz Island ; anchor run out and hove off, and brought up to wait till cleared.

3.30 P.M.—Weather cleared, weighed anchor, and steamed across to Khabarova, and anchored in 5 fathoms.

Tuesday, September 26.

1.30 P.M.—*Orestes* came in.

2.30 P.M.—Weighed anchor, and proceeded in tow by *Orestes*.

Saturday, September 30.

A light south-west breeze, with fine clear weather.

7.30 A.M.—Log showed 162 miles.

12.30 A.M.—Got a pilot at the light - ship and proceeded up the river.

Bar. 30.4. Therm. 45.

6 P.M.—Came to anchor at Archangel.

THE END

Printed by R. & R. CLARK, *Edinburgh.*

Catalogue of Works

of

General Literature

Published by

Mr. Edward Arnold

hé that hatb an art
hatb everpwbere a part.

LONDON

EDWARD ARNOLD

37 BEDFORD STREET, STRAND, W.C.

Publisher to the India Office

Summary of Contents.

Mr. Edward Arnold's
LATEST PUBLICATIONS.

THE BRITISH MISSION TO UGANDA.

By
THE LATE SIR GERALD PORTAL, K.C.M.G., C.B.

Edited, with a Memoir, by RENNELL RODD. With over Forty Illustrations from photographs taken by Colonel Rhodes, engraved from sketches by E. WHYMPER, WARD R. CHESHIRE, and others.

Demy 8vo., cloth, 21s.

POLAR GL

An Account of a Voyage in the yacht *Blencathra*.

By HELEN PEEL.

With a Preface by the Marquis of DUFFERIN and AVA, K.P., and Contributions by Captain JOSEPH WIGGINS and FREDERICK G. JACKSON.

With several Illustrations, demy 8vo , cloth, 15s.

ENGLAND IN EGYPT.

By ALFRED MILNER,
Formerly Under-Secretary for Finance in Egypt.

New and Cheaper Edition, with a prefatory chapter on Egypt in 1894 by the Author.

Large crown 8vo., with Map, cloth, 7s. 6d.

COMMON-SENSE COOKERY.

By COLONEL KENNEY HERBERT ('WYVERN'),

Author of ' Culinary Jottings,' ' Fifty Breakfasts,' etc.

A standard work on the management and economy of the kitchen, containing full directions as to the best methods of cooking and serving dinners, etc., with a great variety of recipes and menus.

Large crown 8vo., cloth, 7s. 6d.

MISTHER O'RYAN:

An Incident in the History of a Nation.

By EDWARD McNULTY.

A powerful story of Irish Life by a new Author.

Small 8vo., elegantly bound, 3s. 6d.

Uniform with ' Stephen Remarx.'

THE DRAUGHTS POCKET-MANUAL.

By J. GAVIN CUNNINGHAM,

Editor of 'Boys' " Chess and Draughts Corner,"' etc.

A complete handy guide to the rules and best methods of play for beginners and students.   A large number of carefully-selected games are given ; and the English, Italian, Spanish, Polish, and Turkish forms of the game of draughts are explained and illustrated.

A Companion Volume to the Chess Pocket-Manual.

Small 8vo., cloth, 2s. 6d.

Catalogue of Works

OF

General Literature

PUBLISHED BY

Mr. EDWARD ARNOLD,

37 BEDFORD STREET, STRAND, LONDON,

Publisher to the India Office.

1894.

VOLUMES OF REMINISCENCES.

SEVENTY YEARS OF IRISH LIFE. Being the Recollections of W. R. LE FANU. Third Edition, one vol., demy 8vo., 16s.
With Portraits of the Author and J. SHERIDAN LE FANU.

'It will delight all readers—English and Scotch no less than Irish, Nationalists no less
than Unionists, Roman Catholics no less than Orangemen.'—*Times.*

RECOLLECTIONS OF LIFE AND WORK. Being the
Autobiography of LOUISA TWINING. One vol., 8vo., cloth, 15s. With
Two Portraits of the Author.

'There is much to interest our readers in this autobiography. Miss Twining looks
back over her work and the changes that have passed over society with the calm reflection
won by long experience.'—*Guardian.*

RIDING RECOLLECTIONS AND TURF STORIES. By

HENRY CUSTANCE, Thrice Winner of the Derby. Second Edition, one vol., 8vo., cloth, 15s. With a photogravure frontispiece, and eight other full-page illustrations.

. Also a large-paper edition, 21s. net.

' An admirable sketch of turf history during a very interesting period, well and humorously written.'—*Sporting Life*.

ECHOES OF OLD COUNTY LIFE. Recollections of Sport,

Society, Politics, and Farming in the Good Old Times. By J. K. FOWLER, of Aylesbury. Second Edition, with numerous illustrations, 8vo., 10s. 6d.

. Also a large-paper edition, of 200 copies only, 21s. net.

' A very entertaining volume of reminiscences, full of good stories.'—*Truth*.

THE MEMORIES OF DEAN HOLE. With the original

illustrations from sketches by LEECH and THACKERAY. New Edition, one vol., crown 8vo., 6s.

' One of the most delightful collections of reminiscences that this generation has seen.'
—*Daily Chronicle*.

STUDENT AND SINGER. The Reminiscences of CHARLES

SANTLEY. New Edition, crown 8vo., cloth, 6s.

' A treasury of delightful anecdote about artists, as well as of valuable pronouncements upon art.'—*Globe*.

WORKS BY CANON BELL, D.D.,

Rector of Cheltenham and Honorary Canon of Carlisle.

POEMS OLD AND NEW. Crown 8vo., cloth, 7s. 6d.

' Canon Bell's place among the poets will, we feel sure, be finally settled by this volume. In the amount of his workmanship, in the variety of it, and in the excellence of it, he makes a claim which will hardly be disputed for a place, not simply among occasional writers of poetry, but distinctly for a place among the poets.'—*The Record*.

THE NAME ABOVE EVERY NAME, and Other Sermons.

Crown 8vo., cloth, 5s.

' A series of sermons which will prove a model of excellence in preaching.'—*The Rock*.

WORKS by the DEAN OF ROCHESTER

(The Very Rev. S. REYNOLDS HOLE).

A LITTLE TOUR IN IRELAND. By AN OXONIAN. With

nearly forty illustrations by JOHN LEECH, including the famous steel frontispiece of the ' Claddagh.' Large imperial 16mo., handsomely bound, gilt top, 10s. 6d.

' Leech's drawings comprise some of that artist's happiest work as a book illustrator.'— *Saturday Review*.

ADDRESSES TO WORKING MEN FROM PULPIT AND

PLATFORM. One vol., crown 8vo., 6s.

' The orator is a happy combination of the divine and the man of the world—thoroughly in earnest, but looking at everything with the eyes of one who knows what men are and what life is.'—*The Globe*.

THE MEMORIES OF DEAN HOLE. With the original

illustrations from sketches by LEECH and THACKERAY. Twelfth Thousand, one vol., crown 8vo., 6s.

' One of the most delightful books of the season.'—*Athenæum*.

A BOOK ABOUT THE GARDEN AND THE GARDENER.

With steel plate frontispiece by JOHN LEECH. Second Edition, crown 8vo., 6s.

' A delightful volume, full, not merely of information, but of humour and entertainment.' —*World*.

A BOOK ABOUT ROSES. Twentieth Thousand. Crown

8vo., cloth, 2s. 6d.

' A perfectly charming book.'—*Daily Telegraph*.

WORKS BY PROFESSOR C. LLOYD MORGAN, F.G.S.,

Principal of University College, Bristol.

ANIMAL LIFE AND INTELLIGENCE. With forty illustrations and a photo-etched frontispiece. Second Edition. Demy 8vo., cloth, 16s.

'The work will prove a boon to all who desire to gain a general knowledge of the more interesting problems of modern biology and psychology by the perusal of a single compact, luminous, and very readable volume.'—Dr. A. R. WALLACE, in *Nature*.

ANIMAL SKETCHES. With nearly forty illustrations. New Edition, one vol., crown 8vo., cloth, 3s. 6d.

'One of the most delightful books about natural history that has come under our notice since the days of Frank Buckland.'—*The Guardian*.

THE SPRINGS OF CONDUCT. Large crown 8vo., 3s. 6d.

'The material is so well arranged, and the views so lucidly expressed, that the work constitutes a most interesting epitome of modern thought upon psychology and ethics.'— Dr. G. J. ROMANES, F.R.S., in *Nature*.

WORKS BY EDWARD BROWN,

Lecturer to the County Councils of Northumberland, Cumberland, Hampshire, Kent, etc.

POULTRY KEEPING AS AN INDUSTRY FOR FARMERS AND COTTAGERS. With fourteen full-page plates by LUDLOW, and nearly fifty other illustrations. One vol., demy 4to., cloth, 6s.

'The most useful book of the kind ever published.'—*Farming World*.

PLEASURABLE POULTRY KEEPING. One vol., crown 8vo., cloth, 2s. 6d.

'This handbook is as useful as it is comprehensive.'—*Scotsman*.

INDUSTRIAL POULTRY KEEPING. Paper boards, 1s.
A small handbook chiefly intended for cottagers and allotment holders.

'The book is one of very easy reference, and ought to be in the hands of not only every farmer, but also of all cottagers throughout the country.'—*Newcastle Journal.*

WORKS BY RENNELL RODD.

POEMS IN MANY LANDS. Crown 8vo., cloth, 5s.

'It is hardly rash to say that of the younger poets none exhibit a truer love of Nature, or a more intimate knowledge of her phenomena.'—*Academy.*

FEDA, with other Poems, chiefly Lyrical. With an etching by
HARPER PENNINGTON. Crown 8vo., cloth, 6s.

'The descriptive passages possess the delicacy of vision that springs only from intimate and reverent communing with nature. Few readers of Mr. Rodd's poems can fail to be touched by its purity and grace.'—*Saturday Review.*

THE UNKNOWN MADONNA, and Other Poems. With a
frontispiece by W. B. RICHMOND, A.R.A. Crown 8vo., cloth, 5s.

THE VIOLET CROWN, AND SONGS OF ENGLAND.
With a frontispiece by the Marchioness of Granby. Crown 8vo., cloth, 5s.

THE CUSTOMS AND LORE OF MODERN GREECE.
With seven full-page illustrations by TRISTRAM ELLIS. 8vo., cloth, 8s. 6d.

WORKS OF FICTION.

THIS TROUBLESOME WORLD. A Novel. By the Authors
of 'The Medicine Lady,' 'Leaves from a Doctor's Diary,' etc. In three vols., crown 8vo., 31s. 6d.

'An extremely vigorous, well-constructed, and readable story. It abounds from first to last in clever contrivance and thrilling interest.'—*Daily Telegraph.*

DAVE'S SWEETHEART. By MARY GAUNT. A Story of

the Australian Goldfields. In two vols., crown 8vo., 21s.

'From the opening scene in the tin store at Deadman's Flat to the closing page we have no hesitation in predicting that not a word will be skipped, even by the most *blasé* of novel-readers.'—*Spectator.*

THE TUTOR'S SECRET. (Le Secret du Précepteur.)

Translated from the French of VICTOR CHERBULIEZ. One vol., crown 8vo., cloth, 6s.

'An admirable translation of a delightful novel. Those who have not read it in French must hasten to read it in English.'—*Manchester Guardian.*

HARTMANN THE ANARCHIST; or, the Doom of the

Great City. By E. DOUGLAS FAWCETT. With sixteen full-page and numerous smaller illustrations by F. T. JANE. One vol., crown 8vo., cloth, 3s. 6d.

'A very remarkable story, which is supplemented by really excellent illustrations by Mr. F. T. Jane.'—*World.*

LOVE LETTERS OF A WORLDLY WOMAN. By Mrs.

W. K. CLIFFORD, Author of 'Aunt Anne,' 'Mrs. Keith's Crime,' etc. One vol., crown 8vo., cloth, 2s. 6d.

'One of the cleverest books that ever a woman wrote.'—*Queen.*

THAT FIDDLER FELLOW : A Tale of St. Andrew's. By

HORACE G. HUTCHINSON, Author of 'My Wife's Politics,' 'Golf,' 'Creatures of Circumstance,' etc. Crown 8vo., cloth, 2s. 6d.

'A strange history of hypnotism and crime, which will delight any lover of the grim and terrible.'—*Guardian.*

STEPHEN REMARX. The Story of a Venture in Ethics.
By the Hon. and Rev. JAMES ADDERLEY, formerly Head of the Oxford
House, and Christ Church Mission, Bethnal Green. Small 8vo., paper
cover, 1s. ; elegantly bound, 3s. 6d.

' It is brilliant, humorous, pathetic, trenchantly severe, sound in intention, grand in
idea and ideal.'—*Manchester Courier.*

GIFT BOOKS.

WINCHESTER COLLEGE, 1393—1893. Illustrated by
HERBERT MARSHALL. With Contributions in Prose and Verse by OLD
WYKEHAMISTS. Demy 4to., cloth, 25s. net. A few copies of the first
edition, limited to 1,000 copies, are still to be had.

' A noble volume, compiled by old Wykehamists, and illustrated by Herbert Marshall
in commemoration of the 500th anniversary of the foundation of the oldest public school
in England. Lord Selborne discourses eloquently on Wykeham's place in history. . . .
" Wykeham's Conception of a Public School," by Dr. Fearon is most interesting : the
Dean of Winchester writes of Wykeham's work in the cathedral; old traditions and
customs are treated of by T. F. Kirby, the Rev. W. P. Smith, A. K. Cook, and others,
while the Bishop of Salisbury contributes " Hymnus Wiccamicus," and the Bishop of
Southwell, Canon Moberley and other writers supply appropriate poetry, all the verses
being inspired with that intense love of his old public school which distinguishes a true
Englishman.'—*Daily Telegraph.*

GREAT PUBLIC SCHOOLS. ETON — HARROW — WIN-
CHESTER — RUGBY — WESTMINSTER — MARLBOROUGH — CHELTENHAM
— HAILEYBURY — CLIFTON — CHARTERHOUSE. With nearly a hundred
illustrations by the best artists. One vol., large imperial 16mo., hand-
somely bound, 6s. Among the contributors to this volume are Mr. Max-
well Lyte, C.B. ; the Hon. Alfred Lyttleton, Dr. Montagu Butler, Mr. P.
Thornton, M.P. ; Mr. Lees Knowles, M.P. ; his Honour Judge Thomas
Hughes, Q.C. ; the Earl of Selborne, Mr. H. Lee Warner, Mr. G. R.
Barker, Mr. A. G. Bradley, Mr. E. Scot Skirving, Rev. L. S. Milford,
Mr. E. M. Oakley, Mr. Leonard Huxley, and Mr. Mowbray Morris.

' No one who has been, is, or expects to be at a public school should be happy till he
gets it.'—*Westmorland Gazette.*

ROUND THE WORKS OF OUR GREAT RAILWAYS.

LONDON AND NORTH-WESTERN WORKS AT CREWE. MIDLAND RAIL-
WAY WORKS AT DERBY. GREAT-NORTHERN RAILWAY WORKS AT
DONCASTER. GREAT-WESTERN RAILWAY WORKS AT SWINDON.
GREAT-EASTERN RAILWAY WORKS AT STRATFORD. NORTH-EASTERN
RAILWAY AND ITS ENGINES. NORTH BRITISH RAILWAY WORKS.
With over one hundred illustrations. The papers are in nearly every case
contributed by officials of the Companies, and the illustrations from official
photographs. One vol., crown 8vo., 3s. 6d.

'Their authors are well-known men; the essays are well written and well illustrated
from official photographs. This interesting little work will be read with pleasure by both
railway men and the travelling public.'—*Railway Herald.*

Volume X. of THE ENGLISH ILLUSTRATED MAGAZINE.
October, 1892—September, 1893. With nearly one thousand pages, and
one thousand illustrations. Super-royal 8vo., handsomely bound, 8s.

'Decidedly the best and most continuously readable of any volume of its class. . . .
This volume is richer in its contents than any of those that went before, and is in the
best way fitted to secure universal approval.'—*Irish Times.*

WILD FLOWERS IN ART AND NATURE. An entirely
new and beautifully illustrated work, to be completed in six parts. By
J. C. L. SPARKES, Principal of the National Art Training School, South
Kensington, and F. W. BURBIDGE, Curator of the University Botanical
Gardens, Dublin. Each part contains three or four beautiful coloured
plates of Flowers from water-colours specially drawn for the work by
Mr. H. G. MOON. In order to do full justice to the plates and enable the
Flowers to be represented in their full natural size, each part is printed
on royal quarto paper, and enclosed in a stout wrapper. Price of each
part, 2s. 6d. Subscription to the six parts, 15s. post free. It is intended
to publish the complete series in one volume, handsomely bound for
presentation, in cloth gilt, price One Guinea.

'The lithographic representations of these flowers (in Part I.) in colour are very successful, and the work promises to be an attractive as well as useful one.'—*The Field.*

WINE GLASSES AND GOBLETS of the Sixteenth, Seven-
teenth, and Eighteenth Centuries. By ALBERT HARTSHORNE. With
many full-page plates and smaller illustrations. In course of preparation.

THE CHESS POCKET-MANUAL. By G. H. D. Gossip,
Author of 'Theory of the Chess Openings,' etc. A complete handy guide to the rules, openings, and best methods of play. Small 8vo., cloth, 2s. 6d.

'Combines brevity with fulness perhaps more successfully than any similar work to be had.'—*Pall Mall Gazette.*

FIFTY BREAKFASTS. Containing a great variety of new
and simple Recipes for Breakfast Dishes. By Colonel Kenney Herbert ('Wyvern'), Author of 'Culinary Jottings,' etc. Small 8vo., 2s. 6d.

'Colonel Herbert's book is one of the best of its kind, for it is thoroughly practical from beginning to end.'—*Speaker.*

HISTORY, PHILOSOPHY, AND SCIENCE.

ENGLAND IN EGYPT. By Alfred Milner, formerly
Under-Secretary for Finance in Egypt. New Edition, crown 8vo., with map, 7s. 6d.

'An admirable book which should be read by those who have at heart the honour of England.'—*Times.*

MY MISSION TO ABYSSINIA. By the late Sir Gerald
H. Portal, K.C.M.G., C.B., Her Majesty's Consul-General for British East Africa. With photogravure portrait, map, and numerous illustrations. Demy 8vo., 15s.

'The dangers to which the mission was constantly exposed, and the calmness and courage with which they were faced, are simply and modestly recorded, whilst we obtain also much light as to the habits and characteristics of the Abyssinians as a nation.'— *United Service Institution Journal.*

THE POLITICAL VALUE OF HISTORY. By W. E. H.
Lecky, D.C.L., LL.D. An Address delivered at the Midland Institute, reprinted with additions. Crown 8vo., cloth, 2s. 6d.

'It should be read by all students of history and political science.'—*Cambridge Review.*

THE CULTIVATION AND USE OF IMAGINATION. By
the Right Hon. GEORGE JOACHIM GOSCHEN. Crown 8vo., cloth, 2s. 6d.

'The book is full of excellent advice attractively put.'—*Speaker.*

THE RIDDLE OF THE UNIVERSE. Being an Attempt
to determine the First Principles of Metaphysics considered as an Inquiry
into the Conditions and Import of Consciousness. By EDWARD DOUGLAS
FAWCETT. One vol., demy 8vo., 14s.

'We are agreeably impressed with the intellectual power and philosophical grasp of
the author, as well as with the evidence of his high literary attainments. . . . The first
part of the work is critical, and lucidly sets forth the landmarks in the history of modern
philosophy : this is exceedingly well done. . . . One of the best parts of the book is that
devoted to the criticism of materialism.'—*Westminster Gazette.*

LOTZE'S PHILOSOPHICAL OUTLINES. Dictated Portions
of the Latest Lectures (at Göttingen and Berlin) of Hermann Lotze.
Translated and edited by GEORGE T. LADD, Professor of Philosophy in
Yale College. About 180 pages in each volume. Crown 8vo., cloth, 4s.
each. Vol. I. Metaphysics. Vol. II. Philosophy of Religion. Vol. III.
Practical Philosophy. Vol. IV. Psychology. Vol. V. Æsthetics.
Vol. VI. Logic.

'No man of letters, no specialist in science, no philosopher, no theologian but would
derive incalculable benefit from the thorough study of Lotze's system of philosophy.'—
Spectator.

THE SOUL OF MAN. An Investigation of the Facts of
Physiological and Experimental Psychology. By Dr. PAUL CARUS.
With 150 illustrative cuts and diagrams. Large crown 8vo., cloth, 12s. 6d.

'A most interesting book, subtle and thoughtful, charged with lofty aspirations.'—
Literary World.

HOMILIES OF SCIENCE. By Dr. PAUL CARUS, Editor of
The Open Court, Author of 'The Soul of Man.' Large crown 8vo.,
cloth, 6s. 6d.

'This book may be read with intellectual and moral profit.'—*Manchester Guardian.*

POLITICAL SCIENCE AND COMPARATIVE CONSTITU-
TIONAL LAW. By JOHN W. BURGESS, Ph.D., LL.D., Dean of the
University Faculty of Political Science in Columbia College, U.S.A. In
two volumes. Demy 8vo., cloth, 25s.

'The work is full of keen analysis and suggestive comment, and may be confidently
recommended to all serious students of comparative politics and jurisprudence.'—*Times.*

THE MARK IN EUROPE AND AMERICA. A Review of
the Discussion on Early Land Tenure. By ENOCH A. BRYAN, A.M.,
President of Vincennes University, Indiana. Crown 8vo., cloth, 4s. 6d.

HARVARD HISTORICAL MONOGRAPHS. Vol. I. The
Veto Power : Its Origin, Development, and Function in the Government
of the United States. By EDWARD CAMPBELL MASON. Demy 8vo.,
paper, 5s. Vol. II. An Introduction to the Study of Federal Government.
By ALBERT BUSHNELL HART, Ph.D. Demy 8vo., paper, 5s.

BETTERMENT. Being the Law of Special Assessment for
Benefits in America, with some observations on its adoption by the London
County Council. By ARTHUR A. BAUMANN, B.A., Barrister-at-Law,
formerly Member of Parliament for Peckham. Crown 8vo., cloth, 2s. 6d.

' Should be read by every ratepayer of the Metropolis.'—*St. James's Gazette.*

THE LAW RELATING TO SCHOOLMASTERS. A Manual
for the Use of Teachers, Parents, and Governors. By HENRY W. DISNEY,
B.A., Barrister-at-Law of the Inner Temple. Crown 8vo., cloth, 2s. 6d.

' This manual should be in the hands of every schoolmaster.' *-Law Journal.*

SIX YEARS OF UNIONIST GOVERNMENT, 1886-1892.
By C. A. WHITMORE, M.P. Post 8vo., cloth, 2s. 6d.

' Not only of ephemeral but of lasting interest.'—*Dublin Evening Mail.*

'MODERN MEN' FROM THE 'NATIONAL OBSERVER.'
Literary Portraits of the most prominent men of the day. Two volumes
in the series are now ready. Crown 8vo., paper, 1s. each.

' All of these sketches are good, admirable alike for the matter and the manner in which
it is put, and show a faculty for judging men which is uncommon in these days.'—*Graphic.*

A GENERAL ASTRONOMY. By CHARLES A. YOUNG, Professor of Astronomy in the College of New Jersey, Associate of the Royal Astronomical Society, Author of *The Sun*, etc. In one vol., 550 pages, with 250 illustrations, and supplemented with the necessary tables. Royal 8vo., half morocco, 12s. 6d.

'A grand book by a grand man. The work should become a text-book wherever the English language is spoken, for no abler, no more trustworthy compilation of the kind has ever appeared for the advantage of students in any line of higher education.'—*Professor Piazzi Smyth.*

PLANT ORGANIZATION. By R. H. WARD, Professor of Botany in the Rensselaer Polytechnic Institute. 4to., flexible boards, 4s. This volume consists of a synoptical review of the general structure and morphology of plants, clearly drawn out according to biological principles, fully illustrated, and accompanied by a set of blank forms to be filled in as exercises by the pupils.

'The order of its arrangement, and the fulness and clearness of the printed hints and directions which introduce the main section of the book, render it a work of high value to a beginner in the study of botany, and of great use for classes.'—*Scotsman.*

A HISTORICAL GEOGRAPHY. By the late Dr. MORRISON, New edition, revised and largely rewritten by W. L. CARRIE, English Master at George Watson's College, Edinburgh. Crown 8vo., cloth, 3s. 6d.

'The style of the book is as good as its method, making it quite as interesting for mere reading as it is valuable for study and for school purposes.'—*School Board Chronicle.*

BY D. H. MONTGOMERY.

THE LEADING FACTS OF ENGLISH HISTORY. With Maps and Tables. Crown 8vo., cloth, 6s.

'A clear and intelligent idea of the main facts of English history in connection with the social and industrial development of the nation.'—*Professor Goldwin Smith.*

THE LEADING FACTS OF FRENCH HISTORY. With Maps and Tables. Crown 8vo., cloth, 6s.

'The right books have been consulted, the facts and views are well up to date, and the language itself is bright and attractive.'—*Educational Times.*

THE LEADING FACTS OF AMERICAN HISTORY. With
numerous maps and illustrations. Crown 8vo., half morocco, 5s. 6d.

'Historical instruction is seldom so interesting in book form as it is in Mr. Montgomery's
"Leading Facts of American History." It is as entertaining as a good story-book, yet
faithful to the author's three chief objects, "accuracy of statement, simplicity of style,
and impartiality of treatment." The numerous woodcuts and maps, some of which are
from old and curious sources, are excellently illustrative of this capital compendium of
American History.'—*Saturday Review.*

THE INTERNATIONAL EDUCATION SERIES.

THE INFANT MIND ; or, Mental Development in the Child.
Translated from the German of W. PREYER, Professor of Physiology in
the University of Jena. Crown 8vo., cloth, 4s. 6d.

ENGLISH EDUCATION IN THE ELEMENTARY AND
SECONDARY SCHOOLS. By ISAAC SHARPLESS, LL.D., President of Haverford College, U.S.A. Crown 8vo., cloth, 4s. 6d.

'The whole of the chapter "The Training of Teachers" is excellent. Excellent,
too, is the chapter on the great public schools—full of keen observation and sound good
sense. Indeed, the whole of the book is as refreshing as a draught of clear spring water,'
—*Educational Times.*

EMILE ; or, a Treatise on Education. By JEAN JACQUES
ROUSSEAU. Translated and Edited by W. H. PAYNE, Ph.D., LL.D.,
President of the Peabody Normal College, U.S.A. Crown 8vo., cloth, 6s.

'The book is well translated and judiciously annotated.'—*Literary World.*

EDUCATION FROM A NATIONAL STANDPOINT. Trans-
lated from the French of ALFRED FOUILLÉE by W. J. GREENSTREET,
M.A., Head Master of the Marling School, Stroud. Crown 8vo., cloth,
7s. 6d.

'The reader will rise from the study of this brilliant and stimulating book with a
sense of gratitude to M. Fouillée for the forcible manner in which the difficulties we must
all have felt are stated, and for his admirable endeavours to construct a workable scheme
of secondary education.'—*Journal of Education.*

THE MORAL INSTRUCTION OF CHILDREN. By Felix

Adler, President of the Ethical Society of New York. Crown 8vo., cloth, 6s.

'A work which should find a place on every educated parent's bookshelves.'—*Parent's Review*.

THE PHILOSOPHY OF EDUCATION. By Johann Karl

Rosenkranz, Doctor of Theology and Professor of Philosophy at Königsberg. (Translated.) Crown 8vo., cloth, 6s.

A HISTORY OF EDUCATION. By Professor F. V. N.

Painter. Crown 8vo., 6s.

THE VENTILATION AND WARMING OF SCHOOL

BUILDINGS. With Plans and Diagrams. By Gilbert B. Morrison. Crown 8vo., 3s. 6d.

FROEBEL'S 'EDUCATION OF MAN.' Translated by

W. N. Hailman. Crown 8vo., 6s.

ELEMENTARY PSYCHOLOGY AND EDUCATION. By

Dr. J. Baldwin. Illustrated, crown 8vo., 6s.

THE SENSES AND THE WILL. Forming Part I. of

'The Mind of the Child.' By W. Preyer, Professor of Physiology in the University of Jena. (Translated.) Crown 8vo., 6s.

THE DEVELOPMENT OF THE INTELLECT. Forming

Part II. of 'The Mind of the Child.' By Professor W. Preyer. (Translated.) Crown 8vo., 6s.

HOW TO STUDY GEOGRAPHY. By Francis W. Parker.

Crown 8vo., 6s.

A HISTORY OF EDUCATION IN THE UNITED STATES.

By Richard A. Boone, Professor of Pedagogy in Indiana University. Crown 8vo., 6s.

EUROPEAN SCHOOLS; Or, What I Saw in the Schools of
Germany, France, Austria, and Switzerland. By L. R. KLEMM, Ph.D.
With numerous illustrations, Crown 8vo., 8s. 6d.

PRACTICAL HINTS FOR TEACHERS. By GEORGE
HOWLAND, Superintendent of the Chicago Schools. Crown 8vo., 4s. 6d.

SCHOOL SUPERVISION. By J. L. PICKARD. 4s. 6d.

HIGHER EDUCATION OF WOMEN IN EUROPE.
By HELENE LANGE. 4s. 6d.

HERBART'S TEXT-BOOK IN PSYCHOLOGY. By M. K.
SMITH. 4s. 6d.

PSYCHOLOGY APPLIED TO THE ART OF TEACHING.
By Dr. J. BALDWIN.

GENERAL LITERATURE.

THE LIFE, ART, AND CHARACTERS OF SHAKESPEARE.
By HENRY N. HUDSON, LL.D., Editor of *The Harvard Shakespeare*, etc.
969 pages, in two vols., large crown 8vo., cloth, 21s.

'They deserve to find a place in every library devoted to Shakespeare, to editions of
his works, to his biography, or to the works of commentators.'—*The Athenæum.*

THE HARVARD EDITION OF SHAKESPEARE'S COM-
PLETE WORKS. A fine Library Edition. By HENRY N. HUDSON,
LL.D., Author of 'The Life, Art, and Characters of Shakespeare.' In
twenty volumes, large crown 8vo., cloth, £6. Also in ten volumes, £5.

'An edition of Shakespeare to which Mr. Hudson's name is affixed does not need a
line from anybody to commend it.'—*Oliver Wendell Holmes.*

THE BEST ELIZABETHAN PLAYS.   Edited, with an Intro-
duction, by WILLIAM R. THAYER.   612 pages, large crown 8vo., cloth,
7s. 6d.

'A useful edition, slightly expurgated.'—*Times.*

THE DEFENSE OF POESY, otherwise known as AN
APOLOGY FOR POETRY.   By Sir PHILIP SIDNEY.   Edited by
A. S. COOK, Professor of English Literature in Yale University.   Crown
8vo., cloth, 4s. 6d.

'A more scholarly piece of workmanship could hardly have been produced. We have
never seen a better student's manual.'—*Westminster Review.*

Leigh Hunt's 'WHAT IS POETRY?'   An Answer to the
Question, 'What is Poetry?' including Remarks on Versification.   By
LEIGH HUNT.   Edited, with notes, by Professor A. S. COOK.   Crown 8vo.,
cloth, 2s. 6d.   This is the first essay in Leigh Hunt's 'Imagination and
Fancy,' which is among the very best of his prose works.

A DEFENCE OF POETRY.   By PERCY BYSSHE SHELLEY.
Edited, with notes and introduction, by Professor A. S. COOK.   Crown
8vo., cloth, 2s. 6d.

SELECTIONS IN ENGLISH PROSE FROM ELIZABETH
TO VICTORIA.   Chosen and arranged by JAMES M. GARNETT, M.A.,
LL.D.   700 pages, large crown 8vo., cloth, 7s. 6d.

'Mr. Garnett has made his selection for the most part with judgment and good taste.'
—*National Observer.*

BEN JONSON'S TIMBER.   Edited by Professor F. E.
SCHELLING.   Crown 8vo., cloth, 4s.

'For strength, sense, and learning, there are not many books in English literature that
can beat this.'—*Saturday Review.*

THE PRACTICAL ELEMENTS OF RHETORIC.   By JOHN
F. GENUNG, Ph.D., Professor of Rhetoric in Amherst College.   Crown
8vo., cloth, 7s.

'A useful and interesting book on a subject that ought to be especially useful and
interesting to an age and nation like our own.'—*Professor J. E. Nixon*, King's College,
Cambridge.

A HANDBOOK TO DANTE. By GIOVANNI A. SCARTAZZINI.

Translated from the Italian, with notes and additions, by THOMAS
DAVIDSON, M.A. Crown 8vo., cloth, 6s. The Handbook is divided into
two parts, the first treating of Dante's Life ; the second, of his Works.
In neither is there omitted any really important fact. To every section
is appended a valuable Bibliography.

'This handbook gives us just what we require—a faithful representation of the man—
his life, his love, his history, and his work.'—*Perth Advertiser.*

DANTE'S ELEVEN LETTERS. Translated and Edited by

the late C. S. LATHAM. With a Preface by Professor CHARLES ELIOT
NORTON. Crown 8vo., cloth, 6s.

' An interesting and serviceable contribution to Dante literature.'—*Athenæum.*

SPANISH IDIOMS, WITH THEIR ENGLISH EQUIVA-

LENTS. Embracing nearly 10,000 phrases. By SARAH CARY BECKER
and Señor FEDERICO MORA. 8vo., cloth, 10s.

' This is a most useful combination of a phrase-book and a dictionary. It gives in
tabular form the various usages of the verbs and other parts of speech most commonly
employed in Spanish. Thus, while many of the phrases might be committed to memory
by one learning the language for colloquial purposes, others will serve to explain the
numerous idiomatic expressions found in Spanish literature.'—*E. Armstrong, Esq., M.A.,*
Fellow and Lecturer of Queen's College, Oxford.

ORIENTAL LITERATURE.

OMARAH'S HISTORY OF YAMAN. The Arabic Text,

edited, with a translation, by HENRY CASSELS KAY, Member of the Royal
Asiatic Society. Demy 8vo., cloth, 17s. 6d. net.

' Mr. Kay is to be heartily congratulated on the completion of a work of true scholarship and indubitable worth.'—*Athenæum.*

LANMAN'S SANSKRIT READER. New Edition, with

Vocabulary and Notes. By CHARLES ROCKWELL LANMAN, Professor of
Sanskrit in Harvard College. For use in colleges and for private study.
Royal 8vo., cloth, 10s. 6d. For the convenience of those who possess the
old edition, the Notes are also issued separately. 5s.

' The publication of the long-expected Notes to Professor Lanman's "Sanskrit Reader,"
completes a work for which every beginner of Sanskrit, and not less every teacher of it
in America and England must be thankful.'—*Classical Review.*

HARVARD ORIENTAL SERIES. Edited, with the co-operation of various Scholars, by CHARLES ROCKWELL LANMAN, Professor of Sanskrit in the Harvard University. Vol. I.—The Jātaka-Mālā ; or, Bodhisattvāvadāna-Mālā. By ARYA-CŪRA. Edited by Dr. HENDRIK KERN, Professor in the University of Leyden, with Preface, Text, and Various Readings. Royal 8vo., cloth, 6s. net.

'The names of Professor Lanman and of Dr. Kern are a sufficient guarantee for the sound and accurate scholarship of this edition of the "Jātaka-Mālā." The Sanskrit text leaves nothing to be desired ; the type is clear and readable, the printing and paper excellent.'—*Asiatic Quarterly.*

Vol. II.—Kapila's Aphorisms of the Sāmkhya Philosophy, with the commentary of Vijñāna-bhiksu. Edited in the original Sanskrit by RICHARD GARBE, Professor in the University of Königsberg.   [*In the press.*

A SANSKRIT PRIMER. Based on the *Leitfaden für den Elementarcursus des Sanskrit* of Professor Georg Bühler of Vienna. With Exercises and Vocabularies by EDWARD DELAVAN PERRY, Ph.D., of Columbia College, New York. 8vo., cloth, 8s.

'It ought to prove a very useful book to beginners of Sanskrit. With its aid students should be able to acquire a practical knowledge of Sanskrit in a shorter time than any other elementary Sanskrit book known to me could enable them to do.'—*A. A. Macdonell, Esq.*, Deputy Professor of Sanskrit, Oxford University.

THE RIGVEDA. The oldest literature of the Indians. By ADOLF KAEGI, Professor in the University of Zürich. Authorised translation by R. ARROWSMITH, Ph.D. 8vo., cloth, 7s. 6d.

'Arrowsmith's translation of Kaegi's "Rigveda" I have found, on comparing two or three passages with the original German, to be perfectly trustworthy. It is a book that every student of the "Veda" should possess, as no other work gives so condensed an account of the "Rigveda," and of the literature bearing on it.'—*A. A. Macdonell, Esq.,* Deputy Professor of Sanskrit, Oxford University.

PUBLICATIONS OF THE INDIA OFFICE AND OF THE GOVERNMENT OF INDIA. Mr. EDWARD ARNOLD, having been appointed Publisher to the Secretary of State for India in Council, has now on sale the above publications at 37 Bedford Street, Strand, and is prepared to supply full information concerning them on application.

INDIAN GOVERNMENT MAPS. Any of the Maps in this magnificent series can now be obtained at the shortest notice from Mr. EDWARD ARNOLD, Publisher to the India Office.

BOOKS FOR THE YOUNG.

MEN OF MIGHT. Studies of Great Characters. By
A. C. BENSON, M.A., and H. F. W. TATHAM, M.A., Assistant Masters
at Eton College. Crown 8vo., cloth, 3s. 6d.

CONTENTS:

Socrates.	Carlo Borromeo.	Dr. Arnold.
Mahomet.	Fénelon.	Livingstone.
St. Bernard.	John Wesley.	General Gordon.
Savonarola.	George Washington.	Father Damien.
Michael Angelo.	Henry Martyn.	

'Models of what such compositions should be; full of incident and anecdote, with the right note of enthusiasm, where it justly comes in, with little if anything of direct sermonizing, though the moral for an intelligent lad is never far to seek. It is a long time since we have seen a better book for youngsters.'—*Guardian.*

THE BATTLES OF FREDERICK THE GREAT; Extracts
from Carlyle's 'History of Frederick the Great.' Edited by CYRIL RAN-
SOME, M.A., Professor of History in the Yorkshire College, Leeds. With
a Map specially drawn for this work, Carlyle's original Battle-Plans, and
Illustrations by ADOLPH MENZEL. Cloth, imperial 16mo., 5s.

'Carlyle's battle-pieces are models of care and of picturesque writing, and it was a happy thought to disinter them from the bulk of the "History of Frederick." The illustrations are very spirited.'—*Journal of Education.*

FRIENDS OF THE OLDEN TIME. By ALICE GARDNER,
Lecturer in History at Newnham College, Cambridge. Illustrated,
square 8vo., 2s. 6d.

A capital little book for children, whose interest in history it is desired to stimulate by lively and picturesque narratives of the lives of heroes, and the nobler aspects of heroic times. Leonidas and Pericles, Solon and Socrates, Camillus and Hannibal, the Gracchi and Alexander, form the subject of Miss Gardner's animated recitals, which possess all the charm of simplicity and clearness that should belong to stories told to children.'—*Saturday Review.*

LAMB'S ADVENTURES OF ULYSSES. With an Introduction by ANDREW LANG. Third and Fourth Thousand. Square 8vo., cloth, 1s. 6d. Also the Prize Edition, gilt edges, 2s.

'Boys in reading the story of the hero's wanderings find in it the same sort of charm that attracts them in " Robinson Crusoe."'—*Manchester Guardian.*

ETHICS FOR YOUNG PEOPLE. By C. C. EVERETT, Professor of Theology in Harvard University. Crown 8vo., cloth, 2s. 6d. OUTLINE OF CONTENTS : Chaps. 1-10, Morality in General : Chaps. 11-20, Duties towards One's self ; Chaps. 21-29, Duties towards Others ; Chaps. 30-36, Helps and Hindrances.

'A series of essays on the generally-recognised virtues and the commoner faults to which the young are liable. It has a truly educative tendency, and is one of a type of book that we should be glad to see more frequently studied in our schools.'—*Guardian.*

A NEW SCHOOL HISTORY OF ENGLAND. By C. W. OMAN, M.A., All Soul's College, Oxford, Author of 'Warwick the Kingmaker,' etc.   [*In preparation.*

RICHARD II. Edited by R. BRINSLEY JOHNSON. Small crown 8vo., cloth, 1s.

A MIDSUMMER NIGHT'S DREAM. Edited by BRINSLEY JOHNSON. Small crown 8vo., cloth, 1s.

These are the first volumes of *Arnold's School Shakespeare*, and will be followed immediately by *The Merchant of Venice, Julius Cæsar,* and other Plays. The text is that of the Globe Edition, through the kind permission of Messrs. Macmillan and Co.

This series is under the general editorship of Mr. J. Churton Collins.

TALES FROM HANS ANDERSEN. With nearly Forty original illustrations by E. A. LEMANN. One vol., foolscap 4to., handsomely bound in cloth gilt, 7s. 6d.

'The artist has entered into the spirit of these most delightful of fairy tales, and makes the book specially attractive by its dainty and descriptive illustrations.'—*Saturday Review.*

BARE ROCK ; or, The Island of Pearls. A Book of Adventure for Boys. By HENRY NASH. With numerous full-page and other illustrations by LANCELOT SPEED. Large crown 8vo., over 400 pages, handsomely bound, gilt edges, 6s.

'A book vastly to our taste— a book to charm all boys, and renew the boy in all who have ever been boys. There are all kinds of delights—a shipwreck, a desert island, a Crusoe-like life enjoyed by two boys, a "surprise party" of savages, and a wonderful coil of exciting incidents among West African blacks.'—*Saturday Review.*

THE CHILDREN'S DICKENS. DAVID COPPERFIELD —THE OLD CURIOSITY SHOP—DOMBEY AND SON. Illustrated from the original plates, and abridged for the use of children by J. H. YOXALL. Square 8vo., cloth, 1s. 6d. each volume.

Also, specially bound for Prizes and Presents, with gilt edges, 2s. each.

'The books have been cut down to manageable length by the excision of passages unsuited to the comprehension of children, or unlikely to maintain their interest, the continuity of the story being preserved by the interpolation of short passages from the editor's pen, printed in italics. The work of compression is judiciously carried out, the type is bold and clear, and the illustrations are taken from the original plates.'—*Guardian.*

'The abridgments of Dickens seem to me excellent. It is the kind of thing that I have always longed for, and that I, in common with many other parents, probably have practically done by skipping while reading aloud. But it is delightful having it in this convenient form, in a book which one can put into the child's own hand.'—*Mrs. Hugh Bell.*

TWILIGHT THOUGHTS—CLAUDE'S POPULAR FAIRY STORIES. With a Preface by MATTHEW ARNOLD. Crown 8vo., cloth, 2s. 6d.

'There is nature and fable and pathos and morality in these stories, something for every taste.'—*From the Preface.*

THE NINE WORLDS. Stories from Norse Mythology. By MARY E. LITCHFIELD. Illustrated, crown 8vo., cloth, 3s.

'These short stories are intended for children, but the author hopes they will not be uninteresting to older persons. We suspect that the latter will enjoy them even more than the former.'—*Journal of Education.*

The Children's Favourite Series.

A charming Series of Juvenile Books, each plentifully illustrated, and written in simple language to please young readers. Special care is taken in the choice of thoroughly wholesome matter. Handsomely bound, and designed to form an attractive and entertaining Series of gift-books for presents and prizes.

PRICE TWO SHILLINGS EACH.

'A charming set of books, which will rejoice the hearts of mothers, teachers, and children.'—*Child Life.*
' Prettily bound, well illustrated, edited with much good sense, and are admirable for presents.'—*Tablet.*

MY BOOK OF FAIRY TALES.

' For children of seven or eight there could not be a better fairy-book.'—*British Weekly.*

MY BOOK OF BIBLE STORIES.

' Written so that the youngest child can understand them.'—*Saturday Review.*

MY BOOK OF HISTORY TALES.

' A splendid introduction to English history.'—*Methodist Times.*

DEEDS OF GOLD.

' A first-rate book for lads and lassies is this. Children cannot but be better for reading such splendid examples of the performance of duty as those illustrated in this book.'—*Schoolmistress.*

MY BOOK OF FABLES.

A very good selection. The morals are rarely more than one line long, the type is large and clear, and the pictures are good.'—*Bookman.*

MY STORY-BOOK OF ANIMALS.

' This book will be found a favourite among the favourites.'—*The Lady.*

RHYMES FOR YOU AND ME.

' It is sometimes thought that slovenly verse is good enough for children, so long as the sentiment and intention are right. The compiler of this volume does not think so ; his choice is seldom at fault.'—*Spectator.*

*** *Other Volumes of the Series are in course of preparation.*

EACH VOLUME CONTAINS ABOUT THIRTY ILLUSTRATIONS.

PRICE TWO SHILLINGS.

PERIODICALS.

THE FORUM. The great success of this Famous American Review, which holds a position in the United States equivalent to that of the *Nineteenth Century* in England, has justified the proprietors in carrying out a wish they have long entertained of reducing its price so as to render it the cheapest first-class Review in the world. With this year its price has been reduced to 1s. 3d. monthly; annual subscription, post free, 15s. A conspicuous feature in the Review is the prominence it gives to articles by European contributors, nearly every number containing articles by the best English writers. It is obtainable in England about the 10th of each month.

'Nothing that I could say would exaggerate my high opinion of the *Forum*, its scope, its management, the ability of its articles, and the importance of its influence.'— *Mrs. Lynn Linton.*

'There is scarcely a number which does not contain one or more striking papers.'— *Ven. Archdeacon Farrar, D.D.*

'In the rank of American periodical literature there can be no doubt that it takes a foremost position.'—*Professor Edmund Gosse.*

THE JOURNAL OF MORPHOLOGY : A Journal of Animal Morphology, devoted principally to Embryological, Anatomical, and Histological subjects. Edited by C. O. WHITMAN, Professor of Biology in Clark University, U.S.A. Three numbers in a volume, of 100 to 150 large 4to. pages, with numerous plates. Single numbers, 17s. 6d. ; subscription to the volume of three numbers, 45s. Volumes I. to VII. can now be obtained, and the first number of Volume VIII. is ready.

'Everyone who is interested in the kind of work published in it knows it. It is taken by all the chief libraries of colleges, universities, etc., both in England and the Continent.'—*Professor Ray Lankester.*

THE PHILOSOPHICAL REVIEW. Edited by J. G. SCHURMAN, Professor of Philosophy in Cornell University, U.S.A. Six Numbers a year. Single Numbers, 3s. 6d. ; Annual Subscription, 12s. 6d.

'Indispensable to the serious student of philosophy.'—*Leeds Mercury.*

AMERICAN PHILOLOGICAL ASSOCIATION, TRANSAC-
TIONS OF THE. Vols. I.—XXI. Containing Papers by Specialists on Ancient and Modern Languages and Literature. The price of the volumes is 10s. each, except Volumes XV. and XX., which are 12s. 6d. each. Volumes I. and II. are not sold separately. An Index of Authors and subjects to Vols. I.—XX. is issued, price 2s. 6d.

MR. EDWARD ARNOLD'S *List of American Periodicals will be sent post free on application.*

L'AMARANTHE : Revue Littéraire, Artistique Illustrée. Dédiée aux filles de France. A monthly Magazine containing original articles by the best French writers, specially intended for the perusal of young people. 1s. monthly; annual subscription, including postage, 14s.

Index to Authors.

www.ingramcontent.com/pod-product-compliance
Lightning Source LLC
Chambersburg PA
CBHW020854020726
47497CB00005B/1402